LIFE and DEATH

The Bristol School of Writing

First edition published 2025 by
The Bristol School of Writing, an imprint of Suspensions Press

thebristolschoolofwriting.co.uk
suspensionspress.co.uk

A catalogue copy of this book is available from the British Library.

Typeset in 12/15pt Garamond

Second impression 2025

ISBN: 978-1-9193532-0-3

Cover image: Death and Life by Edvard Munch 1894

Publication information

This book is edited, produced and published by Justin Lyle and Simon Clarke of The Bristol School of Writing.

Acknowledgements

We would like to thank The Bristol Writing Collective, the Bristol Writers Facebook group and the University of Bristol Writing Short Courses for sharing our call for submissions with their members.

We are also grateful to Mike Manson for his guidance as we conceived this collection and thought about how to publish it. He shared his experience from The Bristol Short Story Prize and the Bristol Review of Books.

Finally, we would like to thank all of the writers who shared their work.

Contents

LIFE AND DEATH

Intro: Clarity, Wisdom, Laughter

The idea for the Bristol School of Writing came out of nowhere, or everywhere. It came up in conversation. Then it resonated with people – now here we are.

The concept is a publication for writers in Bristol and the South West, established and new. A space for the community to come together on the page and in person, to read each other's work: to explore, celebrate and learn.

We are a school of writing in several senses. First, we are a school of writers, like a school of fish, swimming together.

Second, we want to learn from each other, from our strengths and weaknesses, the craft of writing. To this end, a brief "Appreciation" follows each poem and story.

Finally, and most sweepingly, we are a school in that we promote a specific set of literary values. These are expressed in our mantra: clarity, wisdom, laughter.

We think the best writing expands the consciousness of the reader, opens new perspectives that enable a richer, deeper experience of life. Interesting characters, important themes, nuanced thought and feeling embodied in living images. Clear, sensuous language.

We welcomed writing in all forms and on all subjects, and received 60 submissions. Every writer received feedback. We selected 15 stories and two poems for publication. The pieces are ordered in a rough chronology of theme, from the beginning to the end of life, and the collection is entitled Life and Death.

We like all the stories and poems, for different reasons. Our three favourites are Blue, Mollie and The Added Bonus of an Off Switch. Which are yours? And why?

Herring Gulls by Amy Bacon

(*Larus Argentatus*)

Cyclists weave through traffic on Hotwell Road in early morning light as gulls catch thermals over the glistening Avon. They swoop low, then steadily flap their silver-grey wings to soar and glide again – white tail fan and underwing feathers echoing cirrus clouds above.

A few land on the water, bob across wavelets. One heaves a fish his own size and weight to the surface, begins to peck at the fresh flesh. The fish flaps wildly – escapes. The gull repeatedly shallow dives to reclaim his prize while others caw and circle overhead.

Mid-morning on Hannover Quay, builders in fluorescent jackets raise an apartment block behind a silver gridded fence with red safety signs – they install spikes and blue nets on the roof to stop gulls nesting and blocking gutters with grass, twigs and straw.

The gulls arrive on this perfect new island with a steep cliff-face. They balance on the spikes with webbed, tough-skinned feet and build nests anyway – will defend their chicks with vomit, beak and wings.

Lunchtime, harbour-side, outside The Arnolfini, workers emerge from shady offices. They stretch, smoke and sit on benches munching sandwiches from plastic wrappers.

The gulls patrol van rooves, spy with steely, lemon-ringed eyes waiting for dropped crisps and pastry bits. Human hearts flutter as they swoop and dive, pick a fajita left on a wooden table, squabble over burgers and chips spilling from a bin onto the pavement.

Late afternoon in Trenchyard Street, shoppers recoil as one gull kills and tears open a pigeon; she cocks her smooth, white head as she pecks, her bill yellow as the ferryboats carrying tourists.

She flies away – returns to her nest on the roof of a concrete car park to feed her chicks; three hungry bundles of dappled-grey feathers, peeping loudly, instinctively tapping the red spot on her bill for more.

Tomorrow, she'll fly thirty miles to farmland – follow ploughs to find freshly upturned grubs. In the fading evening light, they settle to sleep. A few others fly out to sea to ride the tide.

Appreciation

This beautiful prose poem introduces us to a Bristol of gulls, nurturing and violent. Birds and people are interwoven with equality, in clear, luminous images. We feel the avian atmosphere of the city, the workday, the building site, the harbour, and finally escape to the sea.

Mollie by Karen Lewis-Barned

An ordinary Chertsey Sunday. It is early September 1966 and I am nine. Mollie lives next door in Abbey Gardens, a little estate of houses only built when mum, Avis, was having me. We have black leaded lights and big lawns to play on.

I am sitting tiny behind Mollie's Frigidaire in her kitchen, all ears.

"Just asked him one thing. One simple thing … you'd think even Mike could manage that, wouldn't you, Avis?" Mollie's voice goes up, like her black painted eyebrows.

I can see how really angry she still is with Mike who went off to live in Molesey with another lady, leaving little Nick with her at number eleven.

That loud question just gets left in the air.

My mum doesn't answer for three reasons:

Today she is actually pinned down. She's sitting on one of Mollie's plastic chairs having her hair done as she does most Sunday afternoons. Mollie is doing a 'wash and set' – and I like to think how the sticky setting lotion will help keep my mum's red-brown hair so curly. Mollie is now using the long, pointed tail of a special comb to make neat partings across my mum's scalp like tractor lines across a brown field. She winds each section of wet hair around a big bristly roller, really fast. Ta da! Mollie makes it look easy but then she does spend all week in Norman's fancy salon in Weybridge as a proper hairdresser.

My mum happens to like Mike. I have seen a photo of him playing chess with my dad. Mike has slick hair and is smiling, in a patterned cardigan, tumblers of beer on the low table. He helped my dad, hefting big slabs of rock to make our terrace. For both my parents, Mike is a good bloke.

Mollie is like a television lady giving a sort of show. She is small, brown-haired, with dimples in her cheeks which make her look pretty. I don't think she even wants my mum to answer.

"It's got to be brown lace ups at Wallop. Start-Rites! How can I possibly afford them?" And Mollie picks up a special pin, stabs it into a roller. As if Mike himself is being stabbed right here in the kitchen in Chertsey.

Then she covers my mother's head of rollers with a hairnet and starts a new topic. It's still men. But about my dad now.

"How's Fred anyway?" She has a funny look, staring right into the big wall mirror in front to catch my mum's eyes in the reflection.

"Same really," my mum rolls her eyes.

I think of my dad before we dashed round here.

"Don't be too long at Mollie's," he said from his soft chair. Tea at six." His face did not look friendly.

Mollie is now putting a huge beige dome over my mum and she will sit under it for ages. Mum smiles as she starts to flick through Mollie's *Woman's Realm* and can't be got at by anyone. At the end, a spray of Elnett hairspray from a tall, golden can. This bit makes my eyes itch and gets up my nose, so I creep out through the back door well before it happens.

A few weeks later. I'm looking out of my big bedroom window and I can see my dad and Mollie, on the driveways next to each other, separated by rose bushes. Both off to work.

"Morning Fred." Mollie has a sort of laugh in her voice, trendy in black polo, tight checked skirt.

"Have a good time in the labs!" And while she's speaks, she pulls off high-heeled, fluffy slippers. She pokes about under the front seat of the Mini for Hush Puppies for driving.

My dad does that nod thing, his lips not smiling. He unlocks the door of the Cortina, reverses, up and out of Abbey Gardens to The BP Research Centre at Sunbury-on-Thames.

Then mousey-haired Nick appears in conker-brown blazer with its shield and golden writing on the top pocket, grey shorts, long socks up to his knees, proper leather satchel. He holds onto his cap as he's bustled into the back seat of the Mini by his mum.

"Come on Nick. They'll have your guts for garters if you're late at Wallop!"

And I think about Mollie sending Nick to Wallop in Weybridge, which they call a Prep School. I have seen

Wallop from the car, a grand house made of red bricks, small playground surrounded by old trees with big leaves so it's all shady. I think of my brand-new Chertsey primary school, the high, wide windows, light in straight lines all over the nature table.

"Twelve in my class, all boys," Nick tells me in a voice which is serious and proud.

There are forty-four in my class.

I sometimes imagine how different it must be for Nick at his little wooden desk, doing his Latin. And I know how much Mollie must want this for her son because you have to pay for Wallop. Or Mike does anyway.

"Private schools! Over my dead body!" I see my dad from behind *The Guardian*, a paper tent, as he sits right down into his television chair, feet crossed.

Which makes me think about my mum and dad and how they went to grammar schools, meeting each other at Nottingham university. Mum, Head Girl, getting up at six to do her homework. Now she's a social worker at Ashford hospital, helping teenage girls when they've had babies and there's no dad anywhere and everyone says that's not right.

Mollie was working in a hairdressers at fifteen, she once told me, sweeping cuttings of hair into a dustpan, no exams. She still moans about being on her feet all day even at her posh salon with those Weybridge ladies.

Nick says he wants to be a doctor, like Sarah's dad, Dr Davison, at number fifteen. I think this is exactly what his mum wants and Wallop is part of the plan.

***

October half-term, 1966. Mollie is standing on the kitchen doorstep with an idea.

'How about I take Karen and Nick on a little trip to Bentalls today, Avis?" Mollie's all dressed up, the brass buttons on her little jacket twinkling in the autumn sunshine.

Bentalls, huge department store, supercalifragilistic-expialidocious.

I can't wait.

Nick and me bundled into the back seat of Mollie's Mini. Like she can't get out of Abbey Gardens fast enough. Like she needs to get out now. Straightaway. We curve along the Thames fast, reading the signs – Chertsey, Shepperton, Walton-on-Thames, Hampton Court, Kingston.

And then there's Bentalls: another world.

Or Mollie's world, I think. Nick and me scrunching our noses on the ground floor with all that perfume, made-up assistants spraying Mollie's wrists as we run to the escalator.

And on the first floor, weaving through the shoppers, are living models all in the latest gear, so much taller and thinner than the people I know. Their legs go on forever and they bend their knees so low their strides are enormous. It's like they're floating along – smooth like those new hovercrafts on the television. They never speak, smile or seem to blink so I wonder if these lovely mannequins are *actually* real? Each one carries a card in front of her tummy saying how much you have to pay for a plum Jaeger suit like hers, the coloured tights and pointy shoes.

"Ice cream parlour now, you two. Wafer or cornet? What about a chocolate flake?" Mollie looks cheeky, darts to the front of the queue. The ice cream man in pale cotton coat and hat pushes down the lever of the silver machine, winks at Mollie. I watch soft vanilla – Dulux Brilliant White – magically twirled into Askey's cones. Nick and me spin round on high stools, giggling.

***

Boxing Day. Like every Boxing Day, we go next door to Mollie's party. She has presents for everyone in that thick shiny paper the colour of jewels – red, gold, purple. Paper chains, holly and mistletoe, Mike dressed up as Father Christmas. The lot.

A tall, silver, real artificial Christmas tree stands in what she calls her lounge, and we call the sitting room. It is decorated with lights which flash on and off, tinsel of shocking pink and the neon blue of the fish in our aquarium.

Not like our pine tree. I picture my dad coming downstairs this morning, the green needles on the carpet going sharp into his bare feet.

"Bloody hell!" you could tell he was cross but he looked daft in his pyjamas.

But at Mollie's now the house is filling up, getting noisy, the sudden bang of Nick's indoor fireworks making me jump even though I tell him I'm not scared. She's got the Tarrings from the big old house at the top of Abbey Gardens, Dr Davidson and his lot, of course, and Dr Charley from opposite who everyone tells me invented Ribena. Friends from Weybridge, like Norman.

"Put on Russ Conway, Nick … the Party Pops one," Mollie hands him the LP. And she's off, her small body twisting down low to *Sidesaddle* in her kitchen wearing a velvet shift and a flashy gold bangle.

"Gorgeous top, Karen," she says grabbing my hand to dance along with her. Today she's got on what my parents call her 'telephone voice' which is a bit like the queen but louder. But I feel warm in my tummy to know she has noticed my cream blouse from Harrods with its bell sleeves like Dusty Springfield.

And while I twirl about to Russ Conway I think how Mollie really likes the tinkly music of this very popular pianist indeed. She may actually know him a bit – the way she pointed out his luxury house on the road to Woking one time as if she's been inside. Like she's leant against his Steinway in his bungalow, watched his fingers fly faster, faster, faster over the black and white keys. Or she's met him at a party in Weybridge sometime, maybe even turned his hair into that beautiful, high quiff with Brylcreem.

But it's time to eat and, you should see Mollie's buffet, as she calls it. My mum and Mollie take *Cordon Bleu* every month, watch Fanny Craddock on television with her pencil eyebrows and blond waves. Johnny, her husband in the background, glugging glasses of wine.

Chicken vol au vents, mini prawn cocktails with powdery orange paprika and slithers of lemon on top.

Sticks of cheddar and pineapple coming out of a half grapefruit. And yesterday Mollie borrowed the pink tin salmon mould from my mum and has made an amazing fish mousse. It sits in the centre of the table, dill as seaweed. An olive for the eye, stuffed with a red dot which Mollie tells me is pimento so the fish looks at you sideways, evil.

Next Mollie wheels out a golden trolley on little wheels, bowls of pudding on each shelf. A pavlova with layers of meringue, all gooey in the middle, double cream, frozen raspberries. Black forest gateau, those red blackish cherries, curly bits of dark chocolate on top, more cream inside. Peeled and cut up oranges with dates in a glass bowl, swimming in a syrup stuff made of sugar and brandy. Makes me feel wobbly just smelling it, licking the spoon. Mollie has gone to town.

But there she is, sitting on a top stair with a man I don't know. She is wearing black lacy stockings, thrown off her sling backs. They have plates of food on their knees but don't seem to be eating much at all, more looking at each other and laughing. Because I do know Mollie has boyfriends which means really, really best friends.

***

Later Christmas holidays. I watch Mollie 'put on her face' at the kitchen mirror, a vast glass pane along one wall. Max Factor smoothed all over her face, eyebrows painted, a careful stroke of black eyeliner with a little flick at the end, and no smudges. Stretching her lips to put on a deep, pink lipstick and then sucking them together and dabbing them with a Kleenex. Takes five minutes.

"Be good, the pair of you. I'll only be a mo. There's Tizer in beakers on the glass table in front of the TV – and Twiglets." Mollie slings a black patent bag over her shoulder, darts to the back door.

"See you later alligator!"

"In a while crocodile!"

She's gone.

I sit on the leather sofa, Nick lying on a furry rug right close to the screen. We guzzle all the Twiglets, eyes fixed on *Crackerjack*.

"I'm bored," says Nick. He turns off Leslie Crowther doing his big goodbye smile. He starts running about the house. I can't even keep up when he goes upstairs two at a time.

Then he stands on the landing outside his mum's room. "I can show you something, he says, in there." He's looking right into my eyes.

Go into Mollie's bedroom? That's not right, everyone knows that. And say she comes back?

He pushes open the closed door and I sort of have to follow him. I look at the big bed just for Mollie, the silky pink eiderdown. The long dressing table with mirrors each side like ears, the velvet stool from Lady Penelope's mansion in *Thunderbirds*. Vogue on the little bedside table, not *National Geographic* or *New Society* on each side of my mum and dad's bed.

Nick grabs one of the perfume sprays by her bed. *Diorissimo*. Both of us know the label's foreign so he does a funny voice, "Eau de Toilette." That makes us two snigger and think of toilets. Then he rushes to me near the door, sprays it right into my face. It smells strong and like his mum, but I squint and rub my eyes. Not funny now.

All at once he's sliding open the heavy mirror doors of her wall-to-wall wardrobes. All those clothes! Smart, pressed slacks, mini dresses, short-sleeved satin tops, soft coats – some of them with real fur.

Mollie's like the cut-out doll on the back of *Bunty*, my comic every Saturday morning. Nick's mum has clothes like the tiny ones I cut out so carefully to put on the little paper girl. Bunty, standing so cheerfully there in a sort of swimsuit or vest and pants, waiting for me to make her a really super new outfit. Small, fold over tabs to make the clothes stay on which they never do.

But Nick's not thinking about Bunty. He's got his concentrating face on, lips firmly pressed together. He's digging about under the stilettos. After something special.

"Ah, at last!" he shouts, flinging a pair of white kinky boots across the carpet.

And now I see a pile of magazines which have been hiding, right in the corner. Not the magazines my mum and dad get with their *Sunday Times*. The ones I can see on the high shelf when I go to Littles' newsagents in Chertsey High Street to pay the bill with my mum – *Penthouse*, *Playboy*, *Men Only*. I notice then, my skin prickling, that all have ladies on the front covers who are hardly wearing very much at all.

Nick picks a really special one, waving it about. His thin lips open in a grin but I'm not smiling. On the bed I can see this magazine properly now, and I know – within seconds – what he wants me to see.

Because there's Mollie. Her eyes are laughing, the brown curls look fantastic, the dimples. There's Mollie, sitting on a rocking horse, bare legs each side, the horse's head covering most of her front. There's Mollie with not a stitch on, but cheerful, like Bunty.

My tummy feels odd, like when I have to eat cold, pink custard at school, the little flakes of desiccated coconut on the sponge square sticking in my throat.

"You've gone red," Nick says.

"I'm off," I say. "Tea-time now." I fly down the stairs, hoping my mum and dad don't see how I look, still sicky inside.

***

July 1970. I'm nearly thirteen and standing in the kitchen while my mother sweats over cooking roast beef, Yorkshire pudding and apple pie, my father's favourites and Sunday expectation. Wooden thermometer on the wall says nearly ninety degrees. The door is open so some of the steam from the boiling potatoes, carrots and cabbage can drift out onto the terrace. My mum lifts the heavy lid of the pan over the sink by the window to drain the potatoes, ready for roasting.

"Look outside. Now," she says.

I copy her, swivel my head to look out into the garden. We zoom in on next door's lawn over the low brick wall which separates eleven and twelve Abbey Gardens.

"All right for some!" my mum's face is shiny, strands of copper hair sticking to the sides of her cheekbones.

Mollie lying on a towel, browning like the grass in this Chertsey heatwave. And I think, in her minuscule, psychedelic bikini of swirling pinks and purples, Mollie looks fab.

***

Christmas holidays, 1977. I come home from college and things are different. Now at number eleven, Colin and Sandra, glamorous BA cabin crew. They're always flying from Heathrow to Paris, Colin running round with a baguette to put on our back door mat, navy jacket undone to show the bright red, satin lining.

And Mollie has flown away too. Off with Lars, her Swedish boyfriend, to a huge bungalow with mock Greek columns each side of the front door. Out of Abbey Gardens in Lars' Jaguar to Millionaire's Row in Virginia Water, which is probably even posher than Weybridge.

Appreciation

We are immersed in the perspective of the perceptive girl as she pieces together a portrait of a female social reality of the 60s and 70s. Thick with vivid, telling objects and details, the story brings to light intricacies of class, aspiration and vulnerability in the figure of the resourceful Mollie. Her disappearance from Abbey Gardens evokes the transience of childhood and of the changing times.

The Child by H.T. Greatorex

In 1867 a child was born so beautiful that the following events should not seem peculiar or disproportionate. The child emerged into this cold world in a two-bit, rickety cowshed beneath a passing sungrazer. Folks for miles around saw that purple comet and declared it must be the Star of David.

The midwife cut the cord and yet the child was not placed in a manger for a crib – for in the manger slept a foul-smelling and cantankerous old farmhand who had rented it for seven dollars for the duration of the harvest.

This ill-tempered and odorous man took one look at the baby and drew the ancient pistol that he kept holstered in one boot.

The midwife looked at the baby and she looked at the farmhand. The light of the comet glinted through the patchwork roof of the cow shed and shone on the pistol and shone also on the knife of the midwife. And the midwife and the farmhand gathered up that child and snatched the farm manager's prized mares and galloped clear to the county line before the mother's birthing cries finished echoing around the cowshed.

In those parts, a stolen child was an abomination. A villainous woman was a rare novelty. As the poor mother's outrage rang out across the fields and paddocks, a posse was formed and in many farms that year's harvest wilted on the stalk and horses' hooves went unshod as many a sharecropper or blacksmith's apprentice rode out for glory and revenge. WANTED posters were printed and stuck up in gaols across the state. It being election year, the Governor of that State offered an eye-watering reward for the safe return of the child and the apprehension of the kidnappers.

The midwife was found double-crossed and hogtied in her petticoats in the upstairs room of an abandoned saloon. When the posse took the gag from her mouth, she cursed the farmhand to the rafters with language so foul that every last man and boy blushed and turned away. The child was gone.

On the scaffold they asked her if he made her do it. Asked if they had some devious plan and had maybe lost a child themselves. She only laughed and said of the farmhand things that can't be printed here. Then she said *you fools one minute with that child was worth this fate ten times over* and she nodded to the hangman to do his work.

While the midwife's petticoats still fluttered beneath the gallows, the farmhand was found with a twelve-bore hole in his chest slumped over a display of baroque curtains in an upmarket haberdasher. It was apparent that the rogue had come into town to purchase the finest Egyptian muslin with which to swaddle the child. The store-owner, a family man of great standing in the community, took one look at that child's face and gave the sharecropper two barrels of buck shot in the chest and rode out with the child before the blood had soaked through the thick Persian rug.

From then on, it was heard far and wide that the child's face was kept hidden. All who hunted the pair whispered amongst themselves that to look upon the babe's beauty would lead a man to his grave. And indeed the haberdasher was caught by a patrol of the National Guard. He clutched the babe in his arms as he was chest deep in a flooded gorge wading to freedom. He would have pushed off into the current but for a carefully placed lasso.

The pair were marched to the tent of the Major with the babe in a knapsack. And all the way the haberdasher cursed the gods and not a man among them dared look in that knapsack on pain of a flogging.

The Major was a war hero and a fair man – so famed because like all Majors in that Army he had a feather bed in his tent but unlike all those other leaders of men this Major spent each cold night sleeping on the hard ground next to the bed in solidarity with his men. And because of rumours of the child's mysterious and deadly beauty the child's face was hidden from the men. The haberdasher was left in chains and a guard of the most loyal soldiers stationed at the entrance.

In the morning, the men waited until the sun rose overhead and still the Major had not been seen or heard. When the men drummed up the courage to enter the tent uninvited, they found the haberdasher bled out on the captain's feather bed with a bloody bayonet on the sheets beside him. A hole had been cut from the back of the tent and the Major and child were long gone.

The Major was a man of some means and no small amount of courage and grit. He burned his uniform in a ditch, traded his sabre for a mule, and emptied his family account at the nearest First National Bank. He took to the hills.

After four cold and hard winter months the posse had mostly disbanded – its numbers were cut further with each dead-end and refuted rumour. In November, they came upon a campsite with a broken child's rattle in the embers of the fire. There was a sighting near the Mexican border in January. Not long after, word came that a stevedore in San Francisco swore blind that the Major and the child had taken the slow boat north for the Yukon.

United States Marshall Ingnacious Severn knew different. He sat apart from the others and sharpened his long and pitted bowie knife. The Marshall waited until the trigger-happy deputies and saddle-sore sharecroppers gave up that cold trail and headed home to their disloyal sweethearts and long-failed crops. Then he headed into the mountains.

The Major was found shot through the throat beneath a mountain pass where some ancient flood water had turned and burrowed beneath a mess of tree roots. There the Major had hidden with the child and there in that hollowed out cave the old war hero had made his stand. The mule was long slaughtered and eaten and the hide hung up between two tree roots to deflect the icy wind. About the natural cave were strewn wooden animals carved by hand through the long winter evenings.

Before he left this world, the Major had enough breath yet to condemn Marshall Severn who had shot him in cold blood and taken the child over the ridge and into the valley below.

In the bloodstained diary in his jacket pocket were scrawled reams of poetry on a single topic. Those pages told of a more fragile beauty than the first snowflakes that hover fleetingly over a mountain hot spring and vanish an inch from the surface. A magnificence more stunning than a sudden landslide that swept the very trail from beneath your horse's feet.

Now the posse numbers swelled again. Hunting a child-stealing midwife was a duty. Hunting a disgraced Major was sport, as long as there was a trail to follow. Hunting a Federal Marshall was a jubilee.

In the spring of 1868, the Spokane Kid and all eight surviving members of the Coyote Gang escaped from a Wyoming chain gang leaving behind two dead warders and a half-finished boulevard. They presented themselves at a backwater gaol that evening by the light of burning torches and called for the Sheriff.

When the Sheriff got up the courage to ask for their terms, they demanded to be deputised in the hunt for the missing child. The Spokane Kid and each of his grisly crew spat before they took the oath and each swore he signed up not for Uncle Sam's dollar, but for long-overdue revenge on one Marshall Ignacious Severn who had consigned them to the hard labour to which they found themselves decidedly unaccustomed.

After a decade of their rampant campaign against private property and two years more of toil in the hot sun chained to one another, these outlaws were no longer the baby-faced playboys of two-cent paperbacks. They were grizzled desperados who were known to have shot down men and women alike in the street to make good their many daring escapes.

They had with them a Sioux woman – a scout who could find anything living or dead by reading not only the tracks on the earth but the shape of the clouds above. And although the signs she read were no more than vapour, they caught the scent of their quarry before the cherries ripened on the trees.

The Coyote Gang caught up to Marshall Severn beneath a great elm tree and there, with the babe clucking in her basket, the Marshall knew himself to be cornered. The hard road and nerves had left the lawman a haggard shell. Gone was the once proud performer who smoked cigarillos clenched between his teeth in court and wore the brim of his Stetson folded up on one side like General Custer. Now the Stetson was gone and his nails were chipped and his smile was crooked for missing and blackened teeth. Still, he greeted the Coyote Gang with the courtesy old campaigners should afford one another and sometimes do.

Something smiled in his eyes when those varmints brought out the rope. And although they slandered his name and the name of his parents and shot at the ground near his feet, the Marshall stood unflinching when they put the rope around his neck. Instead he smiled and said only *my fate is yours.*

Because these outlaws were men of grit and iron who sought to test themselves against the laws of the very earth, each one looked upon that child and said nothing. While the Marshall's legs were still twitching, the Spokane Kid drew and shot each of his companions – life-long blood brothers every one of them. And that grizzled outlaw picked up the child, eyes shining, and held the babe to the light to gaze upon her.

When with trembling hands he placed the babe back in its basket, the Sioux scout – who had only played dead – stepped from behind the elm and cut his throat from ear to ear.

The Sioux scout's name was Ehawee. The men who stole the Sioux lands – on which to tend crops, mix cocktails and drive eighteen wheelers – called her *Laughing Maiden*. Ehawee, who hadn't laughed in half a decade, wiped her hands on the trunk of the elm tree until they were clean of the blood of the Spokane Kid and the bark was wet and dark. She stooped before the basket that the Marshall had fashioned as a crib and pulled at the finest Egyptian muslin.

Inside she found more folds of muslin and pulled at these and kept pulling. And from that basket she pulled a bolt of cloth that flowed into her lap and around her ankles and kept coming, yard after yard, and in her haste to see the child again she pulled harder and faster and as the sun sagged overhead the fine cloth gathered around her feet and rose first to cover her ankles and then to her knees.

Ehawee was found by the posse adrift in a lake of finest Egyptian muslin so wide that the great roots of the elm were lost from view and from a mile off the hillside shone white like the first snows. And as the posse pulled at the cloth, they discovered the empty basket and the bodies of the Spokane Kid and the Coyote Gang, while the Marshall twisted on his rope watching on.

Ehawee was tried in front of the local Judge. It was found that since she had been deputised, and because Marshal Ignacious Severn, the Spokane kid and each of the Coyote Gang were wanted men, she had committed no crime.

But in that state at that time the law was not kind to the Sioux and so Ehawee was strung up all the same. She said nothing throughout the trial, nor as she climbed the gallows. The newspapers wrote that her lined face showed not a twitch of the good humour that her name foretold. After a half hour twitching on her rope, her feet still kicked like the living. They cut her down and found her in no better humour, but as alive as ever. And so Ehawee was set free with a handshake and the Judge and the posse patted one another on the back and said *some folks is meant to live*, and *you can't argue with the LORD*.

Ehawee returned to the elm and sat in its roots and spent her days there asking strangers if they had seen the child. A child so beautiful that your heart stopped in your chest and from that day on your blood flowed just from habit. And in all the years she sat out beneath that tree in rain and shine, if she ever drank so much as a sip of water or ate a scrap of bread, no one saw it.

And when that child would have been old and grown, Ehawee was there still. When she passed on it was said that her flesh rotted down amongst those tree roots and amongst the long-rotten shreds of finest Egyptian muslin and her bones mingled with the bones of the animals and birds that had come to know that place as extraordinary.

Appreciation

This post-modernist story plays with the genre and forms of the Western, creating a vibrant and funny world of clichés. It says something about the intoxicating power of beauty, and ventures into magic realism. The tale is driven by the hunt for the stolen baby, a figure of perfect beauty, but finally even the baby is gone. There is no centre, or stable reality, only a kaleidoscope of surfaces, a pursuit.

Poinsettias by Celeste Harvey

The classroom was a workshop of bowed heads and hurrying pencils, childish arms sweeping in time like metronomes, until the thoughtful pause when one colour was exchanged for another, followed by its resumption. A small glistening Christmas tree sat dunce-like in the corner. David sat in front of it, his small dark head focused fiercely on the red and green lines he was making at his desk: tracing paper overlay a William Morris flower which had travelled, in relief, as far as his page. His hand flew up the turgid green stems and gently reddened the velvet tongues of the poinsettia with fluidity and ease.

His first flower finished, he moved his pencil tentatively to its side and began to draw a second flower, free hand, tucking the petals of the second beneath the neat edges of the first. He could barely believe his own quiet audacity — drawing free-hand when there was the tracing paper, with a perfect movable bloom, just finger-widths away. No one else was doing it. He found that this second flower's freedom made him feel masterful and solid, and that, out of nowhere, he wanted to challenge it, and the idea of its perfection, to a duel.

David won. This second one was perfect, just like the first, but it glimmered with a fragility the first one lacked. Looking at it with saucer eyes he felt a lump of feeling rise in his throat. He realised that the flawed second poinsettia looked like a science drawing of his own heart. Seized by an immense and sudden joy he drew more, flower on flower, petal on stem, again and again until the red pulsated with life and his fingers ran with an ecstasy that shocked and surprised him. He had never lost himself like this and found himself again so clearly. This was what he might do whilst the other children kicked balls and celebrated goals, flying around the playground with their shirts thrown up. No more pretending to be interested, or volunteering to act as back-stop so he wouldn't have to bat or stand out-field. He would draw flowers instead and would find the whole world at the end of a colouring pencil. The red and green pencils fit so well, so neatly, into his hand that they became the batons for him to run with, the wands for him to quietly wield. Soon all the white was gone, sunk beneath an ocean of red and vivid green. His classmates worked beside him, unaware of his triumph. David wanted to draw forever, on limitless space, covering the walls and world with his own beautiful designs. Gazing reverently at the original, he felt William Morris reach down through the ages and take his trembling hand.

David's complex sigh caught the attention of the teacher, who raised an eyebrow and a crinkled pearlescent eye. She rose from her creaking chair and made her way over to David. She placed her glasses on her nose and peered over David's shoulder as he held his breath and stared at the flowers planted so vibrantly upon his desk. She exhaled a reproach, then tutted.

"David, I asked everybody to draw one poinsettia so we can display them all together on the notice board. How can I display this many of yours," she asked, pointing at the paper with her soft gnarled knuckle, "when everybody else has just drawn one?"

Disappointed pride smelted anger. David's eyes burnt like coals as he gazed downwards, inwards, threatening to ignite the accused sheet. He could barely breathe for the tightness that gathered round his neck. His hands clenched into fists and he shook her in his mind until she was a rag doll of cotton and creamy powder and he was a giant and an artist and a soul. The teacher flinched when the boy's angry black eyes flicked up to challenge her. From her standpoint above him, his head was wreathed in angry red.

"There's no point getting angry, David. The other children have all done as I asked. Look! Sandy and Adam, and look, Michaela, have all just done one," she said, pointing to the pictures of his immediate neighbours. Without moving his gaze from the plump face of his oppressor, David felt eyes on his back; eyes that would make him pay for this complicated moment with confused taunts and calculated blows. He didn't know how much more he could take; his ribs were already blue from his failures at football and his confidence was like a beetle, crawling and taking cover beneath foliage and divots in the hard grey ground.

He closed his eyes to hide, and found, to his astonishment, red overlain with red. Vast fields of poinsettias to be conquered and explored, stretching out into the distance. A pale sun shone over the blooms of his imagination, pushing colour into the corners of his mind. In that instant David was up on his feet, pushing his chair back into the knees of his teacher. His dumb peers radiated morbid excitement as they watched him throw open the ground-floor window of the classroom and leap from it like an animal, possessed by defiance, the flowers pressed tightly to his chest. The sparkling green grass, turned jade by the frost, rose up to meet him, making light work of his fall. He trusted these colours. As the teacher leaned her bespectacled bosom out of the open window, David disappeared off into the dark woods, in search of glorious red.

Appreciation

This tender, vivid piece captures the moment of a sensitive child's self-recognition as an artist. Such sensitive souls are the poinsettias of the title. Trapped in the standardising institutional setting of the classroom, the boy makes an exuberant literal and figurative escape, leaping out the window.

Speechless by Hilary Smith

"Don't you like your lunch Amy?" She doesn't respond. Not even a flicker. I see there's a dent in the pile of sweetcorn and the slice of ham is ragged at the edges, like a mouse has nibbled it. The rest of the food is untouched.

"She don't speak Miss," Terry says. This isn't news to me, I haven't seen Amy talk to anyone in the two months since I've been here. Unlike Terry, chatting with his mouth full of bright yellow sponge cake, a dribble of pink custard glistening on his chin. These kids love that pudding, can't get enough of it, always queuing up for seconds, thirds some of them. Not Amy though, she barely gets through her main course, let alone dessert.

"She don't eat neither," says Terry helpfully. He's scraped his bowl clean and is already half out of his chair. "Can I go Miss?" He doesn't wait for a reply and is out the door and in the playground before I get a chance to remind him to take his bowl to the trolley.

I should go after him really, Tina would. "You're too soft on them," she says. "You've gotta show 'em who's boss or they'll walk all over you." I glance around the dining hall but Tina and the other dinner ladies, Carol and Misha, have already gone to supervise the children outside. I'm left to chivvy the stragglers and slow eaters. Like Amy.

I start wiping down her table and smile at her. "It's ok if you don't want to eat it love, you can go and play. I'll be out in a minute." She looks up at me and I see what I think is a flash of gratitude in her dark eyes although it's hard to tell. She gets up as cautiously as a rabbit leaving its burrow and takes her plate over to the trolley. She scrapes her unwanted food into the bowl of leftovers with slow deliberation, delaying having to face the playground.

When I've finished cleaning the tables I go outside and find Amy by the door, waiting for me. She slips her hand in mine. "Hello you," I say. "Let's go and find your friends shall we?" But she shakes her head and I let her stay with me right through lunchtime until the bell goes. Having Amy beside me is the best bit of my day.

Tina says I shouldn't indulge her and it's not fair on the other children. "We all have favourites," she says, "you can't help it, some kids are just nicer than others. But if they pick up on it, it causes no end of trouble." She can talk! It's obvious who her favourites are and she's just saying this because she doesn't like it that Amy's attached herself to me and not her. "And her not talking," she says, "that's just attention-seeking. If she was my kid I wouldn't put up with it." And then as if catching herself out, she adds, "not that I don't feel sorry for her, what with her mum and that. But she's been gone, what? Two years now? And her brothers have got over it. They don't have any trouble talking." I grit my teeth. I want to snap at her,

"You stupid woman! Do you know nothing about loss? She's not attention-seeking, she's trying to disappear!" But I don't want to get on the wrong side of Tina or expose my own pain so I smile stiffly and say nothing.

A few weeks later it's the annual school trip and all the staff, including us dinner ladies, are expected to go along. Tina says it's only worth doing for the extra money but I'm happy to spend a day at the seaside with the children, especially Amy. Her teacher, Miss Watson, asks me to keep an eye on her. "Try to get her to join in if you can," she says, "but don't expect her to be very chatty!" She laughs. I think she's as stupid as Tina.

Amy sits next to me on the beach with her knees up, arms wrapped around her legs, quite still. She's looking towards the horizon but I can't read her face, her eyes give nothing away. "Do you want to go and have a paddle?" I ask. She shakes her head. I pick up one of the spades discarded nearby. "Shall we make a sandcastle?" No response. I look over at Miss Watson setting up a game of rounders, telling children where to mark out bases on the sand. Remembering what she said, I say, "That looks fun. Shall we try it?" Amy doesn't move so I stand up and stroll towards her classmates, hoping she'll follow me.

During the rounders game I keep glancing back at Amy. She stays in the same place, staring at the sea, not moving. When it's my turn to bat I'm surprised to find myself caught up in the excitement as the children chant "Come on Miss! Come on Miss!" I whack the ball and run like I haven't in years, bubbles of childish exhilaration bursting in my chest. Soon my calves are burning but I make it to last base without being caught out. Children surround me, cheering and high-fiving me. Smiling, I look across to Amy, hoping she saw. But she's gone.

My stomach drops like a stone. Freezing liquid floods through me. I try to move but my feet are anchored to the sand. With a huge effort I pull myself away from the children and half walk, half run on trembling legs to where Amy and I were sitting. She's not there. I'm frantic now, pulling up and shaking the beach towels, telling myself she could be hiding under them, already knowing she isn't. I scan up and down the clusters of children playing nearby. None of them is Amy. By now my breathing is fast and ragged, my thoughts scattered. I can't do this alone. Tina is sitting chatting and laughing with Carol and Misha. I try to sound relaxed but my voice comes out harsh and shrill. "Have you seen Amy?"

"I thought she was with you," Tina says. I hear the accusation.

"She was, but…" my voice cracks. I'm close to disintegrating so I stop speaking; I can't let all the fragile pieces of me that I've slowly, painfully put back together, shatter into fragments again.

Tina takes charge. "I'll go and tell the others," she says and I watch as she breaks the news to the teachers and other helpers. Instantly alert, they disperse, moving with deliberate calmness amongst the children, asking if anyone's seen Amy.

Terry points at the distant shoreline. "There she is!" He says. Shading my eyes I see the silhouette of Amy's small figure walking into the sea.

"Amy!" I yell and start to run but my feet are slow and heavy as if an invisible force is holding me back, every step sinking in the soft sand. My breathing is laboured and hot, salty tears prick the back of my eyes. I must reach her. I can't lose another child.

At last I'm running on hard, wet sand, pounding to the water's edge. I can see Amy is already up to her waist in the sea. "Amy!" I scream again. "Stop!" She doesn't turn around. I run into the water and start wading towards her but my legs are sluggish against the cold current and the distance between us isn't getting any smaller. She's up to her chest now.

"Stop!" I shout again. My voice sounds tiny and helpless. I plunge under the waves and swim in her direction. When I resurface, she's no longer visible. Blood rushes in my ears.

"Amy!" I cry, uselessly. I thrash around in circles and dive again into the murky silence. There is still no sign of her. I come up, lungs burning. Suddenly she pops out of the water just next to me, like a bobbing cork. I grab her and hold her head up. "It's ok, Amy, I've got you love, I've got you, you're safe now. You're safe." And keeping one arm around her, I kick and pull us back to the shore with what little strength I have left, and drag us onto the beach.

My body is shaking with cold and shock and I hold Amy close, waiting for help to arrive. But Amy isn't shivering, she isn't even coughing or gasping for air. Her eyes are serene and she looks up at me with a smile that lights her whole face.

"I saw her," she says, "I saw your little girl."

I gasp. I can't breathe. I can't focus.
"She waved to me so I went in the sea. She was nice."
Amy reaches up and puts her hands around my neck.
"Don't be sad anymore," she says.
Amy's voice is strong and clear.
I cannot speak.

Appreciation

This neat, compact and moving story creates a series of clear scenes, establishing the setting, pasts and characters of the dinner lady and silent girl, and culminating in a dramatic, visionary, healing reversal of speechlessness. It evokes the redemptive power of companionship in loss.

You Can't Leave That Lion There
by Dylan Spicer

Clifton used to be a dangerous place to live. I know you do not believe me, but it is true. The epicentre of affluent Bristol living once had an underlying threat on every street corner.

There is always a smirk when I tell someone this. An eye roll soon follows. Was the selection of focaccia not varied enough? Was an oat milk cappuccino still an impossible fantasy? What was so rough about living in Clifton?

Well, the problem was the lions.

I appreciate that, confusingly, Asiatic lions lived in Bristol Zoo, which was situated in Clifton. To be clear, I do not mean these lions. That there were once two different kinds of lions within several square miles of central Bristol is a total coincidence.

Clifton lions tended to be fatter. They had access to rubbish bins, scraps from restaurants, wrappers from the ice cream van. This eclectic diet swelled their bellies with an ocean of plastic and metal. Their mouths were gummy mountain ranges of chipped and missing teeth. Those old

Georgian paving stones are cracked for a reason. Years of abuse from the paws of chubby lions.

Thanks to this lack of proper nutrition their backs were patchy wastelands of pink skin and dull fur. Their eyes had a yellow, rheumy look, and rather than striding with the majestic gait of the king of beasts, they pottered around like summer drunks.

I know this sounds ridiculous. Lions in Clifton? How could you buy designer knitwear when there was a risk of getting mauled? But like most things in life, the extraordinary becomes mundane when it surrounds you. The lions had more than enough food from their garbage buffet to keep humans off the menu.

You had to be careful, but if you saw one coming, you moved across to the other side of the road. Lovely wide roads in that part of the city. More than enough room to fit a human and a lion.

And in those days, there was less reason to visit Clifton. It was a place for weekly banking trips, posting letters, or on special occasions popping out for a curry. Lions often sat in the back alley near the curry house, lapping up masala from a rusty bucket.

There were a few close encounters.

When I was younger I hung around with a girl named Laura, and her little brother Malcolm. I was never a fan of Malcolm. He refused to wipe his nose, wore jumpers on hot days, and gave me strange, mistrustful glances. We sometimes headed to the park, to see if we could spot a lion.

Laura led these expeditions. That day had been a success. The lion lay out in the sun, flicking away flies with a swoosh of a ratty tail. Laura circled around our mark, hands out for balance. A large sleepy eye flicked open, then reduced to a sliver.

"Go and give it a pat Malcolm," Laura said. She cartwheeled on the grass, already bored. Kids in Clifton paid more attention to the magpies than the lions.

Malcolm stepped back, trying to hide behind inch-tall grass.

"Come on Malcolm, don't be a cowardy custard," Laura said. "Give the lion a pat."

Malcolm looked at me, eyes hoping for support. I stared at my shoes. Laura was the reason I was here.

"Just pat the lion, Malcolm!" she said.

Malcolm advanced closer, the lines of his mouth drawn into a grim mask. He paused one last time.

"Malcolm. Pat the lion."

We expected him to rub a scaly patch of skin. Stroke the split ends of the tail. But he shot a grubby hand into a thatch of ragged mane, enough to make those groggy eyes flip open.

It was not that bad. Malcolm went to hospital. They bandaged him up, and sent him home within two weeks. At least now he had some bandages to wipe his nose on. He never needed fingerless gloves again. Laura did not even get in trouble. People were more chilled out with their kids in those days.

The lions started vanishing about twenty years ago. Clifton grew into a hub for business and leisure. Once the tables of the coffee shops spilled out onto the pavements, you could not have lions stealing the hot drinks.

No one announced a cull. No one sent in the troops. Instead subtle changes made all the difference. A new range of council waste bins with a reinforced lid defeated curious paws. Restaurants kept their food scraps in the kitchen. Fences appeared in front of any gardens with warm, cosy hiding places. Weeks went by before you saw a lion. Then when you did, you realised how weird it was that lions existed in Clifton in the first place.

Laura and Malcolm moved away. Their money went a lot further in the countryside.

I last saw a lion in my teenage years. She lay under a scrubby bush on the rim of Victoria Park. I thought it was a dead body at first. Thick ribs poked through loose pink skin. A fly rubbed its hands together on the corner of a sandy eye. I lay my hand on its belly, and counted the breaths. We sat together for a while.

The lions are gone now. Relegated to the sun-faded photos on the walls of pubs. A cleaning company painted claws on the side of their van. A local brewery stuck a lion on their logo. The monocled animal sat at the bar with a pint of stout.

Clifton is no longer a dangerous place to live. You can brunch in peace without your chorizo hash falling prey to sharp teeth. But sometimes I miss the sense of danger, and the sound of paws on tarmac.

Appreciation

This light and funny fantasy paints a portrait of Clifton in bright colours. It centres on the magnificent image of these scraggly lions. Its tone is sharp and comic, as Malcolm is goaded to pat the lion, loses fingers, and his sister doesn't get in trouble because parents were more relaxed in those days. It plays with the theme of gentrification and creates a joyous, quirky parallel reality.

Open Mic
by Richard Owen Collins

There's no waiting list for the open mic. There's no background check. There's no seminar to sit through, no feedback questionnaire to fill out. No application form which must be completed in black ink and block capitals. There's no ID required.

There is a sign-up sheet, but there's no registration or administrative fee. There's no signing up for an account, no entering your email, no creating a password that must be at least 16 characters, alphanumeric, with at least one capital and one special and one glyph and one emoji. There's no captcha, no selecting of the boxes with traffic lights in them.

To get the chance to come to this place, stand up (or sit down, if you prefer) and perform something, in a public space, full of people you probably don't know, all you need is the wanting. It's open. You don't need great skill, or much confidence. Actually, those things would be a hindrance.

That's what's most on my mind, the 'open' bit, as I walk through the door of The Oxford, in Totterdown. It's Sunday afternoon. It's the Open Mic. Everyone's welcome.

I get there early, and sit down at the back with a beer. It strikes me, as I look around the place, at the beer coasters stuck all over the walls, the arthouse paintings of musical figures – Tupac, Biggie, Lemmy – that this kind of place, while not exactly rare, is precious. This kind of place, the 'open' place, is the last true democracy. There's no real money to be made here. The environment is unspoiled. The host, Graeme, in his trucker hat and sunglasses, is setting up. He's been running this thing for nearly a decade now. It might've started as a way to gain some extra cash to support his wife and newborn, but now it's about more than just making ends meet. It's an entire lifestyle.

I mean there's the free beer he gets as host, for one thing, but then there's also the thing itself.

"We're so lucky to have the amount of talent, with the regulars, who're here every week, and then you've got, like, this constant stream of new people you haven't seen before," he'll say, when I talk to him later.

I notice the lower half of a mannequin hanging from the ceiling, dressed in low jeans and blue trainers. I'll learn that newcomers always take a moment to notice it, suspended there as if it was the body of a real human, stuck in the ceiling. Graeme sits on the stage with his electric acoustic, the house guitar, and a woman he'll introduce as his wife joins him. He's ready to open the show. There's about twenty people here, which is either not many or really quite a lot, depending on the context, and anyway, the area around the stage is small and enclosed and quite intimate, so the place feels pretty much full.

On the table in front of me there's a man dressed in a fur coat. He's afternoon drunk, shitfaced, trying determinedly to make a hand-rolled cigarette, with one eye closed, discarded bits of Rizla around the table.

Graeme and his wife open the show with a few medleys of hip hop songs, *Gold Digger* mixed with *Jump Around*, *Baby Got Back* mixed with *Bump and Grind*. It's lively, bouncy, fun, and the audience responds. The drunk guy is on his feet now, having forgotten about his attempted cigarette, dancing, his finger pointing in the air. It's a good start.

I'm at the back, making notes, wondering how I look.

They finish their set, to enthusiastic cheers, and next up on the stage is a group of five older men, dressed in shirts and shoes, with their own instruments: two guitars, a bass and a harmonica. They'll play for the next hour, a host of different blues and folk songs. While they play, I'll notice a picture of one of the men, the harmonicist, hung up on the wall. They're hardcore regulars, veterans of the place, and it becomes apparent they've booked their slots next to each other's, so they can effectively play an hour set as a full band. They're all very competent, which is surprisingly unenthralling as a spectator, and my mind wanders.

This thing is about the openness of course, and the chaos of that is its most appealing factor. Anyone, literally anyone, can get up, and do anything. That is inherently thrilling. It's a little bit like the pot-luck sifting of the charity shops or car boot sales; you might find anything, and what you do find will be unique, and very much unpolished.

To me, I think as I get another beer and the blues group continues, that feels like an antidote to the modern landscape of entertainment, where there's a million bands and TV shows and films and they're all clean and they're all professional and they're all sterile.

I'm reminded of a live performance I was invited to recently, by the hipster YouTube musician Jacob Collier: a highly skilful and talented multi-instrumentalist who packed out Lloyd's amphitheatre. He was good, and that's pretty much all there was to say about it. But watching people be good at things, in this century, when there's lots of people being good at things, is surprisingly dull. Watching virtuosity without the vulnerability, talent without the expression: it's unmoving. You need the human imperfection, the mistakes, the nakedness, otherwise it's just like watching a piece of AI-generated art.

I'm thinking now, as the band plays through their blues set: this thing is also about the mic part. The microphone. The sound system, the amplification. This might sound obvious, tautological, not even worth mentioning, but it feels like I've only just noticed it. This is a place to be heard, literally and symbolically. Everyone gets their fifteen minutes. It's the gateway, to take your creativity out of your bedroom, out of your head, into the streets, where it belongs.

The blues group plays their last song, which one of the members, bald and bespectacled, introduces by saying he's been playing this song all his life and he's never going to stop. A few of the audience members know it and sing along. Next up to the stage is a man and woman, forty somethings, possible spousal combo. The man has a bowler hat and a saxophone. The woman is wearing sunglasses. They receive a warm reception while the man sits on the stool and fiddles with the saxophone. He seems to be having some trouble with it, so the woman starts without him, singing a cappella. She's nervous. Her voice is shaky as she sings a version of *Return to Sender*. The audience shows their encouragement, clapping and trying to sing along with the awkward timing. The man continues to fiddle with his saxophone. The woman finishes the song, turns back to look at the man, who still isn't ready, it seems, he's still there fiddling with his saxophone, not even looking up, so she launches into the next song, *Signed, Sealed, Delivered*, in the same quivery voice, her eyes wide and bright, terrified, and the audience continue with their approval, and I'm completely mesmerised.

I've never seen anything like this before.

If I open Spotify or YouTube, I know more or less exactly what I'll get, but here, I have absolutely no idea.

They move onto their third number, and the man is still just fiddling with his saxophone, and I wonder if it's actually malfunctioning in some way or if this is all part of the act, if this is some avant-garde experimental piece, to subvert audience expectations.

They finish to applause which isn't the least bit ironic.

I get another beer, enjoying myself now, and then next up is a thirty-something woman who plays comedy songs on guitar.

She sings, "I've done New York, San Francisco, most of Mexico … But I don't know where the footpath goes at the end of my road." … and, "Everything's fine everything's normal, I didn't get punched in the face today … But when I drink I want to die'.

The audience knows her, and knows her original songs, and sings along to them, and laughs in the right places.

I'll talk to her afterwards, and she'll tell me that she loves this place. She didn't know anyone when she first arrived, but now she's surrounded by friends. She wrote all her songs years ago, had kids, raised them, and now comes here every Sunday to be part of this.

Then the man behind the bar, the guy who's served me my last three beers, takes to the stage. He gets an enthusiastic welcome as he hugs Graeme, who gets up on stage with him, with his guitar. The barman is going to sing. He has his phone in his hand, from which he reads lyrics. He sings Coldplay, in a nervous, almost apologetic voice, and the audience gives him that same encouragement, which, perhaps because I've had a few beers, warms me, makes me sentimental, and stirs another line of thinking in me.

There's another unique feature of this environment: it's this, exactly this, how the participants are audience-facing, but the audience themselves are part of it. They're not just there to spectate, they're as much a part of the performance as the performer. (This'll become even more true later, as a woman in the crowd will start singing along with one of the performers; it'll be unclear if he appreciates it, but he won't challenge it; it's part of the unspoken rules.)

This is something collaborative, and this, which again might seem stunningly obvious but seems to occur to me freshly, as if for the first time, is an inherent part of creativity itself. It's a social thing. Sure, there are the romantic images of the tortured genius, living in reclusion, hiding in a cabin in the mountains, composing their masterpiece, but I wonder, has that ever actually happened? Has anyone ever created something lasting without the interaction, nurturing and feedback that only other people can give? Maybe the final moment of creation occurs alone, but that's neglecting all the moments like this, where the person stands up and works through something and lets other people help them shape it.

As Cziksentmihayli said: "...creativity does not happen inside people's heads, but in the interaction between a person's thoughts and a sociocultural context." And my mind is turning now, loose and fluid, and as the nervous barman moves on to the next song, I'm thinking about the need most people have now to do this, to participate, to be on the stage, even if it's only for fifteen minutes, even if it terrifies them. It's not enough to just be a consumer. Everyone has things they want to say. They want to produce. They want to create. I'm sure it wasn't always like this. I'm sure it's a product of individualism, of the West. I'm not sure it's entirely without its downsides, but I am, at least in my current state, glad that there are arenas like this where that need can be gratified, even if only temporarily.

And then it's almost as if the night knows what I'm thinking, because as the nervous barman leaves to rapturous applause, the biggest of the night so far, the next person on stage is a young East Asian guy with a guitar.

"Hello, uh, I'm new to Bristol. I moved here from Cambridge, where I did my PhD, but … I've been writing songs for the last few years, and, I don't know, I thought maybe I could do something with it. I wanted to get out of science. I thought…"

"What'd you do the PhD in?" The drunk guy in the fur coat shouts out.

"Physics."

The drunk guy in the fur coat nods his approval, then finally finishes rolling his cigarette.

"Well, I don't know, I have some songs, so. This one is called *Finding My Voice*." The ex-physicist plays, and he's pretty good. It's a fingerpicked song with a soft melody. But rather than listen closely, I just think more about this need so many people have to be seen, to be heard, to create and show their creation. I mean, here is a guy with a PhD from Cambridge, and he's turned his back on that to come play guitar in front of twenty people on a Sunday afternoon.

That says something.

Doesn't that say something?

He plays a couple more, to reasonable applause, and I notice the inverse relationship in these things between virtuosity and level of applause. Like I said, the biggest applause was for the nervous barman, who got such a big applause precisely *because* he wasn't a virtuoso, precisely *because* he was nervous, as if the applause in itself was acknowledging that he wasn't very good, as if it was mostly for his bravery. The more skilled a musician you are, the more confident a performer you are, the less it means. No one comes here to see professional musicians. They can get that anywhere else. They come here for something more, something naked and raw and at times a little bit ugly, but ugly in a beautiful way.

Later I'll talk to one of the regulars, the woman singing along from her seat, and she'll talk to me about this. "They want to appreciate you've come and offered us something very personal. I know when I started, 'cos I used to be an actor, so I sang for my job, I wasn't a confident singer, and especially not as myself, I was fairly nervous starting. But then I knew there was nothing to worry about. There was someone I saw perform, who was very good, really, amazing, but was so afraid of making mistakes, and I think I didn't have quite so much fear of that, because I knew I wasn't, like, great, so I didn't need to protect that. I'm humble about it, so I can throw stuff up there. Because the community's so nice, you don't have to worry."

Then there's another act on, another group of four who've strategically placed their sets next to each other so they can play for the next hour, and then it's time for the final act of the night

Graeme introduces him as A Cappella Andy, and he takes to the stage. He has no instrument. He's a middle-aged man, dressed in a shirt and jeans, with a gentle face. He starts singing *Everything I Own* by Ken Boothe, just him and his voice, and everyone starts singing along. Even the people in the other corner of the pub, the quieter bit with those who don't want to watch the performers, start singing along too. Everyone is clapping. The man is smiling widely.

He does a few crowd-pleasers, *Happy Together*, *Country Roads*, and the whole place, bar staff included, sings along with him. It's a little bit wonderful. He's not much of a singer, and his timing keeps going out of sync with the clapping, but it doesn't matter. This isn't about anything except music, music together, and so much of modern music isn't about music, it's about alcohol sales, merchandise sales, fashion, image, but this is about nothing except singing along, everyone finding the same language. (Okay, maybe it's a little bit about alcohol too.)

When he finishes, the place goes nuts, and I hear someone near me say, "I know that guy. He works in the McColl's by my house. I see him every day."

And my heart sings. The mild-mannered shop worker, who stands in his spot every day completing transactions: he's welcome here, and when he gets here, he brings the house down.

Appreciation

This engaging reportage takes us to the open mic, a full-bodied experience, portraying a diversity of characters and performances. Beyond mere documenting, the sceptical, reflective, romantic narrator explores the meaning and appeal of this activity in relation to contemporary concerns: bureaucracy, standardisation, mass media, consumerism, authenticity, community. The piece echoes the concept of this entire collection: a space of creativity and openness.

Bitter Sanctuary by Simon Clarke

I stand and watch the sun climb high over the mountains. My kudali in my hand, I till the thin, dry soil. Above me, the monastery emerges from the rock face, haphazard, rough-hewn, beautiful. Carved from the side of a cliff at the head of a frozen river, the monastery seems eternal, as if it was birthed from the rock, not made by human hand.

It took months to find this place. Unlike other sanctuaries, no roads have been blasted through the mountains to allow the civilised to defile the landscape. I trekked through dense forest, then up through the tree line to the high land, over rock and ice. Only the mani stones I encountered on the way, dotted along the riverbank or piled in small cairns, each inscribed with the mantra of *Avalokiteshvara*, showed that I was on the right path.

I work with the *Tulku* in the garden. He has nothing but his robes and his begging bowl. He is the happiest man I have ever known. Probably the richest. Sometimes I find myself watching him as he works. Trying to absorb his calm, his peace. I envy him. Then it comes to me that my envy is the very thing that is preventing me attaining his state of grace. I must empty my mind. The thrashing thoughts that anchor me to this hateful earth.

The prayer flags flutter on their poles. We sit and drink butter-tea. We rarely speak. There is no need. My *sensei* conveys wisdom in his stillness. In time he rises and picks up his harrow and I rise to join him. We work together and I feel a bubble of joy rise in me, that I should know this peace, this steadiness.

When I arrived here, exhausted, starving, my mind in turmoil, they took me in without question or reserve. In my first days I ran the gamut of emotion, from despair to elation. Now I feel calm.

Among themselves, the order is silent, but the monks do not shun company. There is companionship in their prayers, in their rituals. They do not cling to the gauzy pleasure of the material world. They pray, they serve, and they are content. I crave this. And that marks me out. I must learn to relinquish desire, envy, attachment. Only then can I truly be one of them.

There is great wealth here. In the antique prayer cymbals, the amulets, the ornate statues of the Buddha. The monks are oblivious. Items are precious because they are holy, not for their material worth. But I see they are made of gold and silver; precious stones stud the surfaces. They are very old; collectors in the West would covet them. Yet no one here understands, let alone cares.

I remember the first time I saw the statue in the *Dukhang*. It was stunning. *Dhyana Mudra*, the meditation Buddha, a sheen of soft gold. The surround was studded with sapphires and rubies. Real. Go to the souvenir shops of Kathmandu and you'll find more Buddhist statues and paste gems than you'd ever believe. Buddha standing, Buddha sitting, Buddha touching the earth, Buddha laughing. Laughing at you, with your credit cards and your wide-eyed, drug addled credulity. Like Buddhism is so *true*, it's so *pure*, it's so fucking *spiritual*. Let me tell you about Buddhism. It's hacking at bone dry soil with a rusty pickaxe to try to plant crops. Crops that probably won't grow because the rains don't come. It's waking up to the bell at 4am, sitting in the silent darkness, freezing, while the monks chant their mantra, over and over and over until at last, hours later, they actually start the serious business of praying.

I calm my anger. None of this matters anymore. I work, I eat, I try to meditate. I sleep.

I wake from nightmares – scarlet and white. Endless bodies, faces, dark corridors. Drugs and raves. Darkness and depravity. A blade hisses through flesh and a fountain of red erupts. I am kneeling in blood. The blood rises. It rises to my waist, to my chest, to my neck. I am drowning. I choke and scream. Then the bell sounds and I am free again, waking to the clear thin air. The bleak, beautiful mountains. The dawn bathing the summits in fire. My anger subsides. I am calm.

My journey took months. From the tourist purgatory of Phuket via the travellers' ghetto of backpacker hostels in Kathmandu, to the trance-heads of Goa, with their lurid outfits and hippie skirts, all made in Vietnamese sweatshops by stunted children, poisoned by dyestuff. Tainted bucket drinks at the Full Moon party in Koh

Phangan. Broken glass on the beach. Garbage everywhere. A neon-lit strip mall where bovine tourists graze endlessly. And everywhere the bodies of the damned, writhing in filth, fornicating mindlessly to relentless pounding techno.

How I loved it. I wanted it all. I opened myself to the whole degenerate spectacle. I drank it in, until, inevitably, it consumed me.

I walked among them, the dead-eyed party girls and their strung-out, lank-haired boyfriends, stupefied on psychedelics, staggering over the toxic sand, and I took them to my breast and I nurtured them and gave them succour. In the dim squalor of my hostel room, incense burning in a cheap metal holder, candles guttering in a coffee tin ashtray, they came finally to understand the futility of their desires, as I showed them the razor-sharp purity of mine.

Restless. So restless. I could never bear to linger. Always driven to move on. Along the backpacker trails, following the spoor of youth and drugs and sex. The henna tattoos and the tie-dye T-shirts. Love beads and ankle bracelets. Patchouli and psilocybin. And in the process I left my own hippy trail behind me. Rumours and whispers; urban legend or horror story.

The prayer flags snap in the high, thin wind. Strings of coloured cloth winding around rough poles, stretching between rocks and buildings. Blue, white, red, green, yellow. Always in that order. Blue is the sky; white the air. Red is… no, red is fire. Green for water; yellow for earth. Harmony. Balance. Peace.

I listen to the flags as they whip to and fro, the wind carrying the mantras out into the wretched world. I hear the chanting in the piercing call of the serpent eagle. *Om Ami Dewa Hrih* – the rebirth mantra. My mantra.

The monk was meditating on the beach at dawn when I found him, the purity of his saffron robe in grating contrast to the detritus of mangled plastic and shattered glass. His tranquility mocking the last vomit-streaked stragglers as they lurched unsteadily away. I watched entranced as the sun rose over the water, streaking the gentle waves with gold. The peace he radiated was a balm to my fractured soul. The stillness an antidote to my fevered wandering.

In gratitude, I embraced him on the empty shore, as I had embraced so many others, but this time I felt only calm, only love. His touch promised absolute tenderness. His empty eyes, an infinite compassion. At the exact moment I asked him how I could end the suffering. He could not speak by then, of course. But still I heard his answer. He filled my void with his essence. I knew then where I should go.

And now I am here. I have left the corruption of the past behind. I am born anew, at the summit of the world. Beyond flesh. Beyond emotion. A speck of existence in the infinite cosmos. Ready to leave my body and its desires behind. At times I find myself hoping for nirvana, but I catch myself. I must not hope. I must simply accept the will of the universe. And I must till the soil in my garden.

The backpackers arrive in the late afternoon. By now it is early summer. Their clothes are dirty and worn, as if they have been on the road for months. They carry prayer beads and mandalas. The girl wears tiny shells in her hair. The guys have hippy beards. But I see one wears a Luminox on his wrist, and the henna tattoos are too fresh. There is a distant pulse of rotor blades, and do I catch the faintest scent of aviation fuel in the air as they pass by the garden?

They are made welcome, as is the way of the monks. And after they drink butter-tea and eat dried meat in the refectory, their eager request to see the monastery is granted willingly. My sensei elects to be their guide. I follow at a respectful distance as he shows them the image of the *Bhavachakra*, the Wheel of Life, above the entrance to the complex. He describes how our existence on the wheel is a cycle of life, death, rebirth and suffering that we seek to escape by achieving nirvana.

Outside he points to the great stupa of the monastery, built high on a platform carved out of the cliff, the squat shape representing the Buddha in meditation. Within his belly are held sacred relics of former monks. I watch as the visitors smile and nod, their heads bobbing up and down like puppets. How can no one see that none of this means anything to them?

Finally, in the main hall of the *Dukhang*, ignoring the walls covered with beautiful mandalas and exquisite paintings of buddhas and other divinities, the visitors are presented with the glory of the *Dhyana Mudra*. Is it just I who can see the fierce hunger in their eyes? The monks pray obliviously. My sensei's words of wisdom and enlightenment fall on the ground before them like animal droppings. I can see the darkness in them. They blight the monastery by their presence.

I slip away before they return to the refectory. I need to return to my room, to sit and meditate. I need to suppress my rage and regain the stillness.

The guests do not attend the evening puja, the chanting and silent meditation. They skulk in their rooms. I am tense, on edge. The shell of my composure cracks and flakes as I wait, burning to move, to act. Still, I chant with the monks. We direct our prayers to heaven, but my attention is on the material world.

At last the monks retire and the monastery lights are extinguished. All is still. I close my eyes and slow my breath. My rushing blood begins to quieten. I am composed. Ready. I move calmly along the passage to their quarters. As I approach the door I am pleased that I feel only *Mettā* – love without attachment. There is no hatred, no anger. Nor is there pleasure. All I feel is boundless compassion.

I lift the latch and silently open the door. They turn their faces in surprise – no one is on guard. A foolish mistake. They reach for knives, but I have my sensei's gardening tools. The reaping is quiet, controlled. I save the girl for last. Her eyes still plead with me as I hold her face close to mine, her body off to the side of the room, piled with the others. I kiss her lips gently. It is a farewell of sorts.

I have done monstrous things. But I am not a monster. I did them for love. Eventually they will understand. And perhaps my time on the wheel will come to an end.

In my room, I sit, in lotus. The monks wait outside. I hear them shifting, the rustling of their robes. A beam of moonlight illuminates the motes of dust in the pure air. On my way here I caught a glimpse of my sensei's face. I could have sworn there were tears. Attachment, you see. It is so hard to free yourself from it.

Om shanti, shanti shanti.

Appreciation

This gruesome horror story creates a credible world and an intriguing pathological psychology. The nature of the story is revealed gradually, subverting the reader's expectations of a tale of Buddhist peace and transformation. We read between the lines, retrospectively, to understand the narrator's murderous obsession and path.

Blue by Rachel Bentham

"He was considered one of the world's top cave divers… his most adventurous dives were undertaken when he lived in Bristol, working as a schoolteacher."

Richard Taylor

Alternative quotations from Bristol poets:

"You makes I laff,
you makes I cry.
My life ain't much,
but it ain't nothing, if you ain't in it."

(from 'Steff') by Bertel Martin

"And if the crash comes? I expect
to meet you in the rubble, half a brick
in hand. Here's mine. Together we can build a crack."

(from 'The Way We Are') by Philip Gross

Greg said it, quietly, in the kitchen, almost under his breath;

"Je t'aime …" He meant her to hear. Lotte was peeling onions, dropping them into a huge bowl, lots of little pickling onions. She'd got a sack of them cheap, and they pricked at her eyes but she held her head up, away from the sharp reek of them, fighting the desire to cry. His self indulgence was infuriating – how pretentious; saying it in French. She answered in English, her hands still stripping off thin brown skins, regardless.

"Well I don't." Gruff.

He had a bloody cheek – she did have a boyfriend, after all. Greg sat quietly at the kitchen table, eyes lowered. He had a talent for silence, but Lotte wasn't about to crack. She'd heard him talking to the plummy women who phoned him, his tone similarly wistful. It was what he did. She could feel hot shoots beginning to creep up her neck, so she grabbed the boiling kettle and doused the onions. Blanching, it was called in the preserving book.

He didn't reply.

Steam mushroomed up to the ancient, stained ceiling. It was a shared house; huge, cheap and slowly rotting. Although it was as unkempt as a student house, none of them were students, they were older, probably wackier. The house contained Greg the cavediver, Alastair, who worked in the Natural History part of the Museum, Cath the teacher, and Lotte, who was an artist and therefore very poor. It was like an old farmhouse, but not a farmhouse, with thick stone walls, freezing in the winter, dim and cool in the summer. The owners had gone abroad, and left their family home gently dilapidating, marooned in urban sprawl. The rent was so cheap it had been irresistible. All around the house spread roads lined with tidy thirties semis that had sprung up after the war. The exhausted piano in the hall sometimes tinkled at night. They put it down to mice. Wet suits and oxygen tanks hung in the old walk in larder. The fridge was half full of grass snakes and drowsy adders in plastic icecream boxes, while spiders and butterflies in film canisters filled the egg and dairy sections in the door. Alastair went on collecting missions in the hills between Bristol and Bath, searching for adders under stones in the early mornings, finding spiders in Bickley woods. He kept them in the fridge because the cold slowed them down into something like hibernation.

Then he'd take them out into the garden, helpless and immobile, and arrange them – butterflies perched on flowers, snakes carefully curled among rocks – too cold to do anything but let themselves be positioned for Alastair's camera. He entered the resulting pictures for wildlife photography competitions, and sold them to natural history magazines. Good for his career. Alastair always insisted it didn't do the creatures any harm.

Lotte watched with pursed lips. How wild is a chilled butterfly? Alastair claimed he adored wildlife. He would get quite agitated talking about a mosquito's mouthparts; as a child, he'd made cardboard masks of insect heads. He secretly brought a black widow spider back from abroad, hidden in his camera bag. After he'd done the fridge treatment and photographed it, he released it in the garden. The great British garden spiders ate it, much to his amusement.

In the overgrown back garden, Lotte grew vegetables. In the daytime she took Greg's bearded collie for long walks – miles of paths and pavements beside a crazy, leaping heap of grey spaghetti. Sometimes on her walks she found pieces of wood that she dragged home. Her bedroom was strewn with wood, and things she was making. The lightshade was made of twisted ivy, and a small dead tree was a lamp.

Lotte was recovering her strength – she had just come back from dying. Her skin was paper white, her eyes a deep, deep turquoise. She had been so ill she had almost given in, drifting in and out of consciousness, travelling into the bliss of white space. But at the last ditch she'd decided to let death go instead, decided she had things to do, although nothing would have been easier than to drift away. She had been to the place most people were most scared of, had a good look at it, and let it go. For the time being. So nothing fazed her. Her deep blue eyes had a relentless gaze.

Her boyfriend, Mack, came and growled at the others in the house. He was earthy, solid, unforthcoming. Lotte was increasingly fed up with him. He believed she could save him from his own miserable state of being through the power of love. She doubted it.

While she skinned the onions, to divert Greg from his unwanted declarations, she told him about Klein, her current inspiration; he was the artist who made International Klein Blue; canvases covered solely and solidly with bright, intense blue. The hottest, most cloudless sky, a blue heavy enough to weigh on your chest until you were breathing blue, pure and clean as the air racing through a seabird's lungs. Above the ultimate, most azure ocean. Or the bluest of eyes. She found it hard to explain in words. Sometimes she painted blue eyes onto her wooden constructions, chinks of blue peeping from the knots. For her, blue was spirit; a colour you could fall into and happily drown.

Greg's voice was soft and cautious. To Lotte, it felt like watching a cat licking its smooth coat, while knowing how the tongue would grate on her own skin. Much of the time, she felt like he was trying to impress her. Trying to impress never cut any ice with Lotte. He started talking about his favourite subject; cavediving. Greg and his cavediver friends would gather to loudly relive their underground, underwater close calls; fondly recalling the crawls, the tricky bends, the muddy sumps they had dived through, holding their breath, with no oxygen tanks and barely room to squeeze their manly shoulders through the tight gaps in the rock. They laughed about the mud they had trailed into the pub where they downed their real ale afterwards; how wild they looked, oh, they were so mad... There were seemingly endless conversations about bits of equipment; clips and valves, the best glue for wetsuit seams. Drinking beer and being their own heroes. Nothing wrong with that, she told herself as he talked.

Lotte went caving, sometimes. A gang of them bumping out to the Mendips in an old van, changing into overalls and hardhats in a twilit field, some of them grabbing a last fag beside the muddy entrance. Then one by one they disappeared into an unassuming hole in the ground. She so relished slipping into the not warm and not cold insides of the earth, groping at rock damp as a new baby's head. Sliding and twisting her body through bellying tunnels; downwards and sideways and upwards until all sense of direction was distorted and all that was left was wriggling in dark holes in the ungiving innards of the earth, refusing to be scared, trusting to the sheer force of her own body, her own confidence. And she relied on the others' knowledge of the caves, their odd, scribbled, notional maps, spare batteries and advice about equipment. She was glad to be with them; no one should go caving alone.

Once, there was a lone bat, deep underground, fluttering through the haze in the roof of the cavern in which they were resting, smoking. They didn't know if it was lost. She knew cavediving was even more intense – adding the incredible claustrophobia of underwater; masks and tanks, the dark water holding the cold of elsewhere.

Greg's eyes were blue, but pale. In response to her talk of Klein, Greg showed Lotte his most recent photographs of the Blue Holes, where he had dived in the Bahamas, colourful spreads in the Sunday supplements. Gorgeous aerial photographs of sapphire sea, spotched with the wobbly circles of far deeper blues, the holes disappearing down through the ocean floor. There were insets of Greg himself, and a full-page glamour shot of him in snazzy yellow diving gear, his head torch illuminating a striped fish. He tried to be casual – the Holes were what mattered; he ignored his own image as if it was irrelevant, while his talk of the beauty of the underwater caves ran close beside Lotte's ear, smooth as a strong current. But Lotte knew. She knew that he would find squeals of admiration and consternation deeply gratifying. The most she was prepared to give out was a thoughtful "hmm".

She scanned the text: 'important discoveries of hitherto unknown species…'

"Why is it important to discover a blind shrimp that no one knew was there?" she asked, "Has anyone suffered from a lack of blind shrimps…?"

She was laughing, remaining stoically reluctant to gush. Greg just laughed back. The word "unspoilt" littered the columns, and Greg continued to talk as her eyes flicked over sentences that were presumably purpose-built to attract sponsorship. It didn't attract her. Something about it felt sad and empty. Greg was talking up the difficulties with equipment and local facilities when Lotte cut in –

"So what's this about unspoilt? I don't understand… doesn't all this coverage just encourage people to go there? And then will it be spoilt?"

He shifted on the hard kitchen chair, but warmed to this, still smoothly purring at her side, moving up a notch to the greater gravitas of he who knows more. "The Blue Holes are so deep they still haven't been fully explored," he said. "We need the sponsorship to be able to get over there. It's an incredible system. Other divers have gone so far and stopped. An American diver was lost down there, years ago, never came back. Maybe he got stuck, or disoriented, who knows? Oxygen tanks only last so long. It's completely still once you get deep enough inside the Holes, no current at all, and very poor visibility. You could barely see a yard ahead in some places. Stuff just stays down there, hanging in the water." He shrugged. "Like the dust of ages.

"It was amazing, and yes, more people go there now, maybe because of the publicity. It's inevitable. Of course it's a dilemma… but they enjoy it. Don't they have a right to enjoy it, too? Do you know what? I even came across a Coke can on the last dive – it was disgusting…There's no escape from multinationals."

"So aren't you part of it?" said Lotte, "Aren't you contributing to that?"

Greg shrugged it off. "It's my living. There aren't that many caves to dive… It does have its downside, but since I've got the expertise…not many people can do it. Maybe it's a bit like mountains; because they're there. It's a great feeling – the best."

He sat down at the table with the colour supplements and the onions, pushed some onion skins aside and rested his elbow in the space. "I've probably gone further than anyone into the Holes, mapped out places no one else has seen. Probably. On my last trip, I got into a cavern that no one knew about. Visibility was very poor because of the detritus in the water; as I said, there's no current. When I held out my arm, I couldn't see my hand. I took hold of something that squashed between my fingers. It was the American diver's hand, held together by his wetsuit. He must have been there several years, suspended in the water along with the sediment. Nothing to disturb his body."

Except you, Lotte thought, grimly. She went back to the onions.

She didn't believe in heroes; but she told Greg the photos looked good because they did. His photos won prizes. He started on about the technology necessary for underwater shots, the weight of the cameras, the need for powerful lighting. Lotte peeled, thinking about prizes, undisturbed shrimps, the chilled wildlife in the fridge. And the suspended dead diver – still there, presumably. Curls of shining onion skin piled up on the chopping board.

As winter approached the house grew colder, clammy. The electrics fizzed ominously in the damp walls – there were many reasons why the house was so cheap. The joists under the bathroom were soft, sodden – you could pull out lumps of wood like sponge and squeeze the water out of them. Filling the bath even half full seemed reckless, considering the weight on the rotten joists below… They all left before the winter set in, separated into different lives, relieved. Cath and Alastair became an item, while Lotte and Mack parted company. Lotte got her own place, and, once she'd paid off her share of the bills, the others from the house didn't visit.

Occasionally, Lotte heard something about Greg. More exploration of the Wookey Holes in Somerset, further dives in the Blue Holes. Years later she heard about Greg's last dive, somewhere off the British coast, nowhere exotic. When she heard she felt sorry. She was ironing, listening to the radio. Sorry about her so sure young self.

He had been with younger divers – (maybe he had a job teaching diving, maybe it had come to that). The young divers told the story, their voices sombre and bemused. It was a routine dive; all of them had enough oxygen to return to the surface, but not enough to go further down. Greg must have known that. He was deeper than the others.

Lotte could see the water in her mind as she listened; grey, not blue. He continued to swim downward, turning and gesturing for them to follow. He carried on, going deeper, not waiting. The young divers were upset, desperate – faced with a horrible choice : risk their own lives to try and follow to try get him to come back, or let him go.

The radio presenter's voice was as deliberately soothing as Greg's. Lotte pictured Greg floating in the quiet deeps, fish nibbling his hair. He had beautiful hair. Or lying in the dark at the bottom of the sea, undisturbed, like the Coke can.

They saved their own lives. Below a certain depth, bodies don't float back up. Something to do with the pressure.

Appreciation

Four people are distinct and real to us, living together in this crumbling house. Every word of the story is luminous detail: physical, psychological, atmospheric. The opening quotations set a comic tone the story will play off. Female and male archetypes emerge, comically and seriously, with Lotte, peeling onions, questioning the holistic logic and value of the men's quests to conquer nature, the caves and the creatures, their bringing back trophies in support of a dubious heroism, or vanity. Blue recurs in paint, sky, water and eyes, like a tapestry, and finally in the older Lotte's subtle, ambivalent, wise reflection on her youthful judgement of Greg, the cavediver. He is finally lost in a suicidal journey to the depths beyond the capacity of his equipment, of his own nature, in futility, or desperate obsession. To the limit of his own masculine identity. A melancholy, blue atmosphere, but now in grey water.

The Cleaner by JM Monaco

It wasn't a fetish. Nothing to do with sex or vanity either. "Total liberation," he told me when we parted ways. "I'd do it in the garden, whatever the weather, if it weren't for my elderly neighbours on one side, the young family on the other." So, indoors it was, duster in one hand, mop in the other.

Roger, the naked cleaner, entered my life when everything was falling apart. The first tragedy hit when my sprightly sixty-six-year-old dad died five weeks earlier from a ruptured brain aneurysm. That evening after the funeral, my hot shot Wall Street brother sat with me in Dad's galley kitchen eyeing the ceiling's damp patches and the crumbling sash window frames. With that smirk of his and a wave of a hand, he said, "It's yours. You know I always hated this place. And to be honest, it'll only cause me a tax headache on both sides of the pond."

Considering his condo in Manhattan, family home in New Jersey, summer place in The Catskills, and the old flat he rented out in London, I didn't see any point in arguing. Out of politeness, I tilted my head and set my hand over his. "That's very generous of you, Johnnie. Are you sure?"

He shrugged. "You should take the offer before I change my mind, little sister. I'm sure you and Andrew will be very happy here. You can stop sinking money into renting and live the mortgage-free dream. What's left of Dad's savings can help with repairs." In the light from the kitchen table lamp with its square crimson shade, the shadow that cast over Johnnie's eyes gave him the look of the devil.

Two nights later I stood in the kitchen of our rented one bedroom in Croydon pouring a glass of Merlot. I had just come in from a life-drawing session at the art college where I work, free classes being a big perk of my admin job. I thought about the challenge of fixing up the house where I grew up. Goal setting was something I had been avoiding and the house project was a perfect way to work through grief. Soon my thoughts filled with fantasies of Andrew and I renovating the place and raising our future family there.

At the sound of the front door opening and closing at 9.30pm, I shouted, "You're back late." But there was something about Andrew's silence that stopped me from taking that first sip of the wine. I set the glass down and when I turned, I was shocked to see Andrew, his expression sullen, standing at the doorway. He had not taken off his jacket and his rucksack was still slung over his shoulder.

"God, Andrew. What's wrong?"

He did not answer but lowered his gaze. His lips started to quiver.

My heart pounded as I feared the worst. Did a student at school wrongly accuse him of something? Had he reached a point where he couldn't take the pressures of teaching anymore?

"What happened?"

"I'm sorry, Jen." He lifted a trembling hand over his mouth. "I can't do this any longer."

Reminding myself not to judge, to support my husband in his time of need, I took in a deep breath. "Well, you've been saying you were unhappy there, but isn't it better to wait till you've found another teaching job?"

"It's not work." His gaze met mine as he pulled his shoulders back. "There's no nice way to say this, Jen, but there's someone else. It just happened. We didn't mean to hurt you."

Lesley, the blonde science teacher. The source of the second tragedy. I had met her at the pub one Friday night with Andrew and some of his colleagues several months before. I never would have guessed she and Andrew had been doing unthinkable things in her bed when he told me he was working late all those evenings. When I think of it now, it did seem odd that this pretty thing with a glossy bob went out of her way at the pub to cosy up to me. "We've heard so much about you," she smiled as she took the empty seat next to mine. "Where have you been keeping her, Andrew?"

When I laughed along and said, "Oh, he lets me out every now and then," she slapped his arm. "Naughty boy."

Lesley bought me drinks that night and wooed me with flattering interest.

"So, tell me all about yourself. I want to know everything."

I told her I managed the admin at an art college. "It's a job I can forget about when I leave, but I like being around all the creativity. I did a fine arts degree and still dabble, but it's a tough world, you know, when you need to pay the bills." I finished with a nervous laugh, not sure where to go from there.

"Anything's more exciting than a numbing life teaching science to spotty teenagers." She told me about her fascination with the arts and how she wished she knew more. Before the night was over, she set a date to meet for lunch followed by a visit to the Tate.

"I'm not sure I always get this stuff," Lesley said, squinting her eyes as she pondered the Louise Bourgeois sculpture, Tits. Holding her fist over her heart, she added, "But I know when it does something to me."

I should have suspected something was up when the lunch conversation turned to Andrew. How did we meet? How did he propose to me? Was he a romantic type? Did he ever get moody?

When I caught my breath in the kitchen after the blow of Andrew's confession, I said, "Were you and Lesley screwing when I met her that night at the pub?"

His hesitation said everything. "Come on. Out with it." And then it flowed like a fast-moving river, picking up hazardous sludge along the way.

"It started maybe six months before. We tried to stop, Jen, honest. I can't tell you how many times we tried. And Lesley feels awful about it." His voice cracked. "The last thing we wanted to do was hurt you. You have to believe me."

I held up my hand. "Enough."

"We need to talk about a divorce. I'm going back there tonight. I'll be back on the weekend for my things."

It was Lesley who had told me about Roger the cleaner over lunch on our girly day out. She owned a two-bedroom flat in Streatham, lucky her, and splashed out for a cleaner because she was far too busy working, having sex with my husband and deceiving me to find time to scrub the toilet. Roger was good and cheap. "But he comes with conditions," she whispered. "Every last stitch comes off. Except shoes and socks." Her eyes widened. "Darling, he even does skirting boards and windows!" She insisted on giving me his number. "You never know when you might need someone like him."

I'd forgotten about Roger until I moved into the mess Dad left behind. While his files were in perfect order, Dad had refused to sort the accumulated clutter and grime, shouting me down whenever I suggested he get cleaning help. The extent of the problem hit me that first night after I moved in. I couldn't bear to sleep in Dad's larger bed, so I retreated to my childhood room, curling up on the single divan. The dust on the dresser, side table, window ledges and stale smell from the old shag pile carpet was so bad it triggered my allergies. Later my sleep was disturbed with dreams of water pouring through the ceiling, eels slithering down the walls, and cockroaches the size of rats skittering across the carpet.

The cleaners I rang from adverts at the local bakery couldn't fit me in. In desperation, I remembered Roger. I'm not sure what I was expecting from this man who insisted on cleaning in the buff, but when we spoke on the phone his soft voice reassured me. "I'm sorry for your loss. And a divorce on the way too. Yes, I've done some cleaning for Lesley. I take it she told you how I work. As long as we're clear on that."

Roger was busy but agreed to work extra hours on Saturdays. Deep cleaning was fine, and he offered to help with the house clearing.

On that first Saturday morning Roger arrived with his own supplies, including a vacuum, mop, and bucket. Wearing a grey hoodie and soiled jeans, he stood on the short side at around 5 foot 6 inches with a stocky build. His receding hairline, beard and thick waistline, suggested he was in his late forties.

"I'm embarrassed it's got this bad." I said when taking him through the rooms.

"Oh, I've seen a lot worse. All it needs is a bit of elbow grease. May take some time, but we'll get there."

From Dad's bedroom I watched Roger step into the bathroom and pull off his hoodie and white T shirt in one smooth move. He slipped off his trainers then jeans and folded everything neatly before setting the pile outside the door. As he bent over to take off his fitted black boxers he glanced up and caught me looking. Ignoring me, he carried on then pushed his feet back into his trainers before taking out a pair of yellow rubber gloves. It surprised me when he opened the window wide during that cold day in March. I wondered how his legs and torso had caught the sun as they were a shade darker than the milky area that his boxers had covered. Sturdy as tree trunks, Roger's legs moved swiftly, yet his calves showed no muscular definition. The weight around his abdomen and sides jiggled, as did the bits hanging from his upper arms when he scoured the bath tiles. Humming an unrecognisable tune while he worked, his genitals swayed in sync.

I emptied Dad's clothes from the wardrobe onto the bed but found it hard to take my eyes away from Roger. I wondered if this was the source of Roger's motivation, exposing himself for the gaze of women clients. But on the phone he had said that Lesley, and many other clients, were usually at work when he cleaned. The more I observed him, the more I began to understand my own fascination. This unrestrained body in motion was completely at ease with itself. After a while Roger took a break and closed the bathroom door. I sat on the bed listening closely to the sounds behind the door; the splashes of urine hitting the toilet water, the creaking of the floor with his footsteps, the clearing of his throat, his heavier breathing at intervals, the resuming rhythms of his scrubbing in time with his humming.

Later I made excuses to go downstairs when Roger tackled the kitchen. Again, he put his all into it; huffing and puffing as he leaned into the mop, grunting as he kneeled on the floor, protected by kneepads, to clean the skirting boards. Sweat from his hairline rolled into his brows and the side of his eyes. From the middle of his back, it trickled down to his buttocks. Every now and then he wiped himself dry with a towel. After he left, I walked through the clean spaces, amazed at the progress. I then stood in the kitchen with my eyes closed trying to burn his image, his sounds, the whole of this unfettered man, into my memory.

That night in the living room I took out a small sketchbook and pencils and tried to capture him on paper. A soft 2B pencil was my first option, followed soon after by a harder graphite when I had no luck. I moved onto larger sheets with charcoal, mining thick lines for the darker shaded areas in and around his body. When those efforts didn't create the depth I needed, I grabbed a rubber and attempted to find the white of the surface again. In frustration and with vigorous pressure I tore through the paper. Returning to the hard pencil again, I scribbled furious marks, eventually burning more holes through the image. Still, the result was lifeless. Nothing I did could grasp what I had seen and felt earlier.

Out of boredom I drank a whole bottle of Merlot on an empty stomach. In my drunken state, my mind trawled through a series of my life's failures. My overweight and unpopular school days. My disappointing A Level results. Getting stuck with my third choice for art college. Not being able to sell my paintings after graduation. Andrew leaving me for Lesley, my so-called new friend. My hedge-fund-manager brother pitying me with his share of the inheritance. I bawled when I found a photo hidden behind others on the sideboard in the living room. It was Andrew and I posing with my parents on our wedding day. Tears streamed through my charcoal smudged face. I wiped them with blackened fingers only to jump in shock at the sight of the charred woman looking back at me when I passed the hallway mirror. I screamed my throat raw, smashed the wedding photo against the fireplace, then tore the failed sketches into pieces. Before I fell into bed that night, I groaned while vomiting over the newly sparkling toilet.

"Have you ever done any life modelling for artists? Art Schools?" I asked Roger the following Saturday.

"Not my thing. I like to keep moving."

"You wouldn't sit for me? Just for a bit of sketching. I can pay you extra?"

"I will not sit. I'm here for the cleaning." He sipped at the tea I made him and saw my disappointment. "Right. How about you do the drawing while I work. But discreetly. I don't like distractions."

I took a moment to consider. "It's not my strong point, but I'll give it a try."

"And you can pay me extra."

Roger took up the old carpet in the living room, not accepting my offer of help. From the hallway I peered inside and let my 2B pencil race across the paper almost as fast as Roger worked. My eyes flitted back and forth from Roger to the image. The sketch evolved into a shape reminiscent of a hay bale rolling across a field, the suggestion of a limb or two caught inside. A buzz from the pit of my stomach rose to my hands. I had never sketched this fast before. We exchanged only glances as Roger cleared the pantry, scrubbed the shelves, threw out old tins and boxes of food, cleaned the cooker and oven. When he took breaks to stretch, drink, or wipe himself down, my eyes continued observing, my pencil always moving.

At the close of the day, Roger went to the bathroom and dressed. Back downstairs he massaged his neck and said, "Let's have a look then."

I flipped the pages slowly as I tried to take in everything. What I saw was a mess of frantic swirls but there was an energy in the chaos that roused me.

Roger held his hand to chin, scratched his beard and nodded. "Okay then."

I turned to the final page where I had sketched a few impressions of Roger reaching far inside the mouth of the oven.

He laughed. "Look at that. It's like Jonah getting swallowed by the whale."

These were the only drawings that focused more on Roger's face, shoulders, and arms around the oven door. In one, I had caught a determination in the eyes, the clenched mouth, his mission to cut through years of someone else's neglect. All in a mass of furious marks I made before the moment disappeared.

"I'll need to go at it a bit more next week, but most of the hard work is done," he said, surveying the kitchen.

"Thanks. And thanks for letting me sketch you."

"If it makes you happy," he lifted his brows in surprise. "I can't complain about the extra cash. It'll come in handy when I'm off on hols to Spain with the missus."

I paid him, said goodbye at the door then slumped on the sofa. It dawned on me that Roger would finish the following week and I would have to face the rest on my own. As I looked around, I ran my sock covered feet over the newly exposed wooden floorboards. They were in great shape and never should have been hidden. My gaze lingered at the school photos of my brother and me, little Johnnie and Jen, that still hung on the wall since our childhood days. A photo of my younger smiling mother, the one that looked like she was winking, sat underneath them, next to a later image taken closer to the time of her death three years ago. The sob that escaped me took me by surprise. Trying to gulp it back caused an unbearable pain in my throat and chest, so I allowed myself to cry. What followed a few minutes later was a rage of tearful laughter that carried on so long my jaws ached. When it settled, my body felt lighter, as if it was being carried away in a summer's breeze. I took the sketches out of the book, found masking tape, and arranged them over the wall-hung photos. Returning to the sofa, I propped a cushion behind my head and stretched my legs. I stared at the wall, long and hard, satisfied, at last. As my lids grew heavy, the images began to bounce around the paper, dipping and gliding from one sheet to another. They formed a dance around the faint tune of Roger's humming and found their way into a sweet deep sleep.

Appreciation

This tale of the muse playfully subverts gender expectations, creating a credible and striking psychological story. The family history is drawn swiftly, we feel the anger and disorientation of the narrator after the loss of father and husband. She is sympathetic through her struggles, not a successful artist but someone who loves art and lives in the real world. Roger is a wonderful, fantastical, redemptive figure, helping her clean up her life, practically and psychologically. It's an imaginative and healing vision.

An American Poet in Exile
by Peter Cowlam

The fag end of the news cycle does not always condemn newshounds to the ashen remains of academe, as it did me one afternoon in North August. Notes I had been given were a brief résumé of one of those 'world-famous' poets no one has heard of outside of creative-writing departments, the latter prevalent in American universities, though the trend has traction here.

You'd have thought it helped his cause when his name was an anagram of Bard (he wasn't a Brad by the way). For ease of usage I shall call him Drab, not having asked how he'd come to be transplanted into English soil. He hadn't lost his Tennessee drawl, and was noted for the evangelising zeal he had brought to redbrick campuses the length, breadth, depth, and anything else, of Shakespeare's sceptred isles. Of course, he alone cannot be blamed for the blizzard of demotic verse, catchment that over the last thirty, forty years has been a 'renaissance' in poetry. Nor the accompaniment, an annual procession of unlikely winners boasting beatific smiles, in a festoon of prestige literary awards.

Also in my notes is his tenure as North August's Poet Laureate. Honourably, with academic retirement pending, this is a post he'd resigned, offering up on that sacred altar the following valediction –

But hey. I was sent out
here on drill,
no way I wouldn't go. Knew how to get
away, as rumored,
before the institution
rapped at my door, with a
docent – smoke, moonshine, mirrors

The task was to tease out something about him, because little was known, at least personally. I'd got the commission when prevailing opinion was that he'd open up, now that he'd left the drudgery of academic life. I was assured by now he'd have dropped the mask, so that here was our best opportunity for someone – for a dupe like me – to join that stunted hill-climb prosodists try to ascend by more than halfway. And in passing, I was asked to ignore what was now tacitly accepted – that Rap artists had shown themselves much more inventive with rhyme.

I was given a postcode, and approximate geography as to where in North August he lived, a drive out from the college town he'd said his last goodbyes to ('Knew how to get // away' etc., or see above). A few streets from his home address (so I assumed) was the Conjugal Barista, a tiny, single-fronted coffeehouse where he agreed to meet me, at two p.m. I couldn't miss it. It was opposite

Patels, a family-run store, where you got eggs, bread, veg, all grocery in fact, and lottery tickets. I did due diligence before I set off, with Google street views, in an arc out from the Patels and the barista. My guess was his house was one of the Edwardian mid-terraces, with abbreviated frontage – adequate for the bins and a pushbike – and overgrown with privet. He had probably been careful not to invite students or colleagues there.

But here was my first problem. I arrived ten minutes early at the Conjugal Barista, to find its window whited and a sign saying closed for refurbishment. Next opening was on the monthly meeting of In Barista Poets, with open mic, a local institution Drab had probably initiated. I'd remember to ask, but then forgot it completely once Drab had arrived. He was ten minutes late. I had therefore waited for twenty, a delay I put to random use over at the Patels, parting with cash for a lottery ticket.

First glimpse of my American poet in exile was as sole pedestrian at distance on his home street, a shambling figure disjointed in his gait. His squat appearance grew progressively larger as he neared, and when fully resolved reminded me of my earliest Italian teacher, a big sporty man with broad shoulders, thick-rimmed square-framed glasses, whose speech was scattergun and rapid, yet whose carefully chosen words were a finely chiselled, English enunciation. Drab when he spoke did not compare, apologising neither for his timekeeping nor for it having slipped his mind that the baristas were closed. More astounding than that, he did not seem to know much about North August, where he had lived for how many years, unable as he was to name an alternative venue (or did he hope we'd cancel altogether?).

I told him of a pub round the corner called the Amble Inn, not to be confused, I joked, with Henry VIII's ill-fated wife, or one of them. He looked at me askance. The place when we entered was draped from every hanging space with the flag of St George. Coasters on the small polished tables were of that same rhetoric, in design, legend, and in saturated hues, a red-white-and-blue. A shelf behind the bar was lined with Toby jugs. I had yet to discern what kind of poet's sensibility his was. With that in mind, I judged it possibly not the best moment for an assimilated left-wing intellectual, given we had entered week on week of heightened national consciousness, with a coronation imminent, and political posturing bound up with a carousel of new Tory leaders in and out. No one could have missed the power build-up of ambition, with pledges to control immigration, finally.

He seemed to know it did not do to look irascible at all this knightly romanticism – at least in public places. Drab sat down, if not very comfortably. He did not want alcohol. Luckily a pot of tea for two was possible. I waited at the bar while it was made, and paid. I joined him with the tray. His was a dash of milk, no sugar. I tried to start my examination with a simple question: what would be his last piece of advice for his students, those eager scribes who'd farewell him, doubtless fulsomely, on his last day in the groves of academe?

Well, there were two things. One had to think carefully before accepting honorary doctorates. The dispensing institution, in the breadth, depth and infinitude of its intellectual largesse, always expected something in return. That meant an exhausting round of addresses, lectures, wry observations, delivered from the lectern. You might get away to a certain extent with the same paper offered up ad nauseam, but eventually someone would notice. "Oh, yes, I'd never have thought of that," I said. "So what was the other thing?" The other thing was this, with Drab now in a look more grave than ever, and manfully weighed by the profundity of what was about to be imparted. The best strategy career-wise for the ambitious, emergent writer – the poet in particular – was to make it widely known that the real struggle – persistent, and almost intractable – was the lifelong grapple with impostor syndrome. "You do that then everyone will think you must be the real thing." I had to admit I hadn't thought of that either, but got no further with that examination, for just then, with a clash of batons, someone squeezing a melodeon, and a tinkle of bell pads, a troupe of Morris dancers tumbled in, and in the loudness of its English, hearthside, patriotic calling made further conversation almost impossible.

It was left to me to find somewhere else, given Drab's ignorance of his adopted topography here in North August. I led him through a drear, low-rise, orange-brick industrial complex, where the work life central to it reddened his cheeks and froze his expression. There were fabricators, welders, paint sprayers, warehouse operatives, dispatchers, inter-depot van drivers, a plumber's merchant – in miniature the Whitman gamut. Among all that human agency was a taproom with a sign up for craft beers brewed on the premises, with a tariff for take-outs, while in the adjacent forecourt a forklift had been parked. No to that, said Drab. A street more to his liking was a jaggedness of pavement stalls and awnings, nail bars, a gym, a Turkish barber, a vape store, all of it too busy and nowhere to sit. I took him to a garden centre, where the café was a reverberance of piped music, hollow, and a not pleasant ambiance, he said. We stood in a field, as rain threatened. The clouds parted when at last I got him to a bakery, its housing a repurposed factory in the manufacture once of television tables. There was coffee. There were pastries. There was seating under a slanting Perspex roof, and a breezeblock wall with wisteria growing up. For a moment the sun shone and dappled the cement floor. "Mine," he said, "is a flat white." I got it. I brought it to our table.

"Good," I said. "Now let us begin. Tell me about yourself."

Appreciation

With great concision and a wealth of visual detail, this piece gives us a portrait of both a man and a national moment. The journalist narrator is a wry and savvy guide; the poet's few comments reveal his character and the place of poetry itself in modern life, so that the final, "Tell me about yourself", is almost redundant. We feel the dishevelled poet's weary dislocation.

Sunny with a Moderate Breeze
by Stephen Lang

Katia side-stepped the puddles as she crossed the decking. She wondered what was supposed to be attractive about the seaside in winter. The letting agent had lied to her. It was far from cosy here.

The beach café prided itself on a personalised full English breakfast. Customers ticked the items they wanted on a paper chit and handed it in at the counter. Katia fancied having a modest selection, but the man tinkering with the coffee apparatus looked too absorbed with his toy to disturb. She decided not to order anything for now.

She found a place to sit in the corner and took out *Sunny with a Moderate Breeze*. Katia was careful not to stain the book on the tea-soaked table, although she had more than enough copies. She wanted to look at it in the open, needing to convince herself that the cover design – a cartoon of a young woman in a pink summer dress surrounded by floating flowers – wasn't just a cheap stock image.

"What's this?"

Katia hadn't noticed the woman sitting next to her. Her paisley dress, large floppy hat and steel-rimmed glasses made her look very 1960s, like she'd spent decades rummaging in thrift shops cultivating the image. Katia could detect a scent of lavender. She imagined her having a name befitting her look, such as Belle or Nova.

"Interesting," she said. "*Sunny with a Moderate Breeze*. Sounds catchy enough if romantic comedy's your thing. The design is a little too generic for my taste, though. Never heard of the author. How does the blurb read?"

Katia picked up *Sunny with a Moderate Breeze* and held it tightly, as if it helped to qualify its existence. She scanned the so-called blurb on the back cover, although she'd read it a hundred times before and had committed the words to memory.

"The author? Oh, well, actually, it's me."

"You?"

"It's my book. I'm the author."

Belle – or Nova – lowered her voice to a whisper.

"Congratulations, darling."

Her eyes bore into Katia, scanning for hidden credentials that might qualify her as a writer.

"It's my debut novel. I've self-published. You know, just to get the first one out there. Get myself seen, as it were."

The woman closed her eyes and nodded like Katia had told her the most profound thing.

"Well, someone has to publish it," she said, creaking open a silver case and taking out a thin cigarette.

"I don't think you're allowed to smoke in here," said Katia.

"Then we'll just have to keep it as our little secret. Won't we?"

Belle – as Katia had decided she was more suited to that name – placed the cigarette between her lips and struck a match.

"Tell me. Who are your influences? Who has inspired you to write?"

"Loads of people," said Katia. "Er, Margaret Atwood. Hilary Mantel."

"Oh, you favour the big names. Rock star authors, eh?"

"If you want to call them that."

Belle – the supposed Belle – tutted.

"Paperbacks have a tendency to be flimsy. They don't last five minutes. Your little book not in hardback?"

"No, currently only out in paperback. And available to buy on Kindle, of course."

"Kin-dle," said Belle, savouring the word like it was new to her. "Hmm. Katia De Souza. So that's your pen name?"

"Well," said Katia. "Sort of. De Souza is my ex-husband's name. I've recently divorced, but I decided to keep it. The best thing about him was his name."

"I see. In my day, we hung on to our maiden names for dear life. It made a more honest dust jacket."

"You're a writer too?"

Belle pulled her glasses forward to rest on the end of her nose.

"Why did you come here, Katia De Souza? In the middle of winter? Why?"

"I love Cornwall. I felt that I would find a sense of community here."

"True. There are a few local authors lurking in these parts. More than a few if you look closely. You have to watch out for one or two of them. There's this cheap horror scribe who calls himself Ernest D. Ablo. I mean. Come on."

"It sounds like you don't like pen names."

"No, I no longer flirt with pseudonyms. I'm Deborah Smith. It's on my birth certificate. Simple, but entirely me. Take it or leave it, darling."

She flicked her cigarette ash on the floor.

"And another question for you," she said. "Are you going to aimlessly carry that bag of books around with you for the rest of your life, or are you going to do something positive with it? Courage, darling. It's all you need."

Deborah Smith blew out an enormous cloud of smoke. It hovered in the air, engulfing them both.

"Nice to meet you, Katia De Souza."

***

The Old Bookshop was near the top of the hill, between a post office that was never open and a sorry-looking bakery with a window display bereft of pasties and scones. Katia had never seen anyone going in or coming out of The Old Bookshop, certainly nobody with their arms full of purchases. Maybe this wasn't such a literary town after all.

The entrance was squat and narrow like it had shrunk over time through lack of use. Katia took a deep breath as she lowered her head and went inside.

A display took prominence in the centre of the shop. Hardbacks stood upright on a table in intricate criss-crossing rows. Their positioning gave the appearance of giant dominoes.

The cover of *The Vampire's Chambermaid* bore a black and white photograph. Ernest D. Ablo wore a thin moustache, and his hairline formed a neat widow's peak. He looked rather charming, at least for a cheap horror scribe. The multiple faces on the row of books all gave the same gap-toothed smirk, like something from a hall of mirrors.

Beside Ernest D. Ablo stood the work of Henry H. Hickman, *The Locked Door Unlocked – A Murder Mystery*. Hickman's photograph showed the tell-tale signs of a hastily-taken selfie. One of his white shirt collars was neatly tucked inside his blue crew neck jumper, the other poking out at an angle.

It was as many books as Katia had seen laid out in a Waterstones display. She thought of the latest release of what Deborah Smith would call a rock star author. The number of copies by Messrs Ablo and Hickman in The Old Bookshop suggested few, if any, had sold. Was this really where Katia expected to start a prestigious career as a writer?

"Did you find what you were looking for?"

The man's voice was hesitant, as if he knew there was little hope in receiving a positive answer to the question. His threadbare jumper and faded baseball cap made him look more like a gardener than a bookshop proprietor. Katia wondered if he'd wandered in to shelter from the rain many years ago and decided to stay.

"Well," she said. "I was wondering if I might have something you were looking for."

Katia opened her bag and took out *Sunny with a Moderate Breeze*.

"I'm renting a cottage overlooking the beach. I'm new around here. I'm a writer. Katia De Souza. Could I interest you in stocking a few copies of my novel?"

The lenses in the bookseller's glasses magnified his tired-looking eyes. They were rheumy and bloodshot, indicating a long life devoted to reading. Katia hoped it might be a good sign.

"I'm so sorry," he said. "I'm afraid titles by local authors tend not to sell."

The bookseller sighed as he picked up a copy of *The Locked Door Unlocked – A Murder Mystery*.

"I hosted a signing event for Henry H. Hickman. He supplied the wine and nibbles. He was so nervous he could only hold the pen with both hands, which rendered his signature an unreadable scrawl. He needn't have worried, as nobody turned up. He got sozzled on the Chardonnay, reading random extracts of his book to the wall. I should have known he was the anxious type. *The Locked Door Unlocked – A Murder Mystery*. Why did he have to qualify the genre? No confidence, that's why. Poor old Henry.

Poor old local writers. I suppose I have a tendency to feel sorry for them."

The bookseller returned The Locked Door Unlocked – A Murder Mystery to the table like its only useful purpose was to balance upright. He pulled off his baseball cap and wiped his forehead with a handkerchief, the account of Henry H. Hickman's failed book signing event having exhausted him. Katia turned to leave.

"I'm sure they appreciate you feeling sorry for them," she said.

***

Katia had bought a new raincoat at the weekend, but she knew it would be mad to go out and test it on a day like today. The rain fell in a relentless deluge, but she still felt compelled to brave the coastal path.

She sat in the corner of the beach café to dry off. Katia started talking before she'd even checked to see if Deborah Smith was there. She could detect the distinct scent of lavender.

"Guess what? The Old Bookshop had Ernest D. Ablo out in full glory."

"I bet they did."

Deborah held up a black umbrella. She shook the rain from it perilously close to the adjoining table, although the people sitting there didn't appear to notice.

"He looks like he might be fun," said Katia.

"Fun?"

Deborah opened her silver case and lit a thin, papery cigarette.

"I don't like horror. And I especially dislike his horror."

"I thought his face made him look better suited to comedy, to be honest. And apparently the other local author Henry H. Hickman had some kind of wine-induced meltdown at his book signing event."

"Never mind them. Tell me about you, Katia De Souza. Sell any books? Make any deals? Nibbles and wine?"

Katia sighed. She watched the rain outside as it lashed against the windows.

"I took a bagful of books with me, but the man in The Old Bookshop didn't seem that interested. I got the feeling he was done with local authors. Or done with books in general. There was this prevailing damp, mildewy reek in there. Or maybe *Sunny with a Moderate Breeze* lacks what it takes. The cover. The blurb. Me. Oh, I really don't know."

"Perhaps somebody needs to breathe a little life into that place. I think that's what it's lacking, don't you?"

"It certainly needs that. But it seemed, well, it seemed like it was on its last legs. I think I tried hard enough. Maybe I should explore options in Plymouth or Exeter. Or even Bristol."

Deborah Smith flicked her cigarette ash on the floor.

"The cities will swallow you. Eat you up and spit out your bones. Do you want that? Try a little harder here, darling. It's where you belong."

She tilted her head back and blew out an enormous cloud of smoke. It hung in the air above them like a grey raincloud.

***

A circle of wooden stools sat in the corner of The Old Bookshop. They were covered in piles of yellowing paperbacks, and Katia assumed it was part of a never-ending stocktake.

"Did you find what you were looking for?"

The bookseller squinted at Katia as he tried to place her. His eyes were even more bloodshot than the last time.

"Oh, hello," he said. "It's you."

He pulled off his baseball cap and wiped his forehead with a handkerchief.

"Hello again," said Katia. "I've had some further thoughts about hosting a book-signing event. I'm happy to bring the nibbles. And we can limit it to soft drinks, if you'd prefer."

She watched him fold up the handkerchief. He kept his eyes focused on his shoes.

"Come on," she said. "What's to lose?"

The bookseller shook his head.

"I don't think so. Sorry."

Katia sat on the edge of the stool bearing the least number of paperbacks. She took a moment to study the display of local authors from a different angle.

"What's this?"

Thundery Showers stood hidden behind *The Vampire's Chambermaid*. Katia recognised the face on the cover. The same floppy hat and glasses.

"Good heavens," said the bookseller.

He dusted the book down and sniffed it, like he was expecting the scent of lavender.

"It's something of a collector's item. I'd forgotten I had it."

"Deborah Smith," said Katia. "Another of your local authors?"

"Oh, yes. Belle was our original local author."

"Belle?"

"Well, I knew her as Belle. She flirted with pseudonyms over the years, and that one stuck with me. I'll always remember her as Belle."

"Yes, it does rather suit her."

"I beg your pardon?"

"Nothing. Tell me about Belle."

He held the book close to his chest.

"She ran a writer's community back in the day. I let them meet here every Thursday to exchange critiques. Right where you're sitting now. But I could see as the outsider that it didn't always gel. It was more of a mismatch of talent than dominant personalities getting in the way. Belle was in desperate need of a peer. An equal." He nodded at the book display. "I sensed her frustration with the young upstarts before she left us."

"Left you?"

He handed Katia the copy of *Thundery Showers*.

"I could do a good price?"

***

Katia tried to convince herself that the bookseller hadn't accepted it as a bribe when she bought the rare edition of *Thundery Showers*. He'd struggled to open the till to complete the sale, like it had fused itself shut through inactivity.

Deborah Smith, the original local author. Katia couldn't wait to tell her.

The bookseller had pushed *The Vampire's Chambermaid* over, and the rest of the books had followed, falling one by one like dominoes. Katia helped to clear the table and arrange the display of *Sunny with a Moderate Breeze*.

They agreed to nibbles and wine.

The sun was breaking through the clouds as Katia followed the coastal path. She took off her raincoat and draped it over her shoulder. The wind swept her hair from her forehead in a rush.

"I did it!"

Katia sat in the corner of the beach café. She took out *Thundery Showers* and *Sunny with a Moderate Breeze* and arranged the two books side by side. Katia lowered her voice to a whisper.

"Deborah, I'm a local author! Just like you!"

She opened *Thundery Showers* and read the introduction. It would be insulting to think of it as a blurb.

Deborah Smith (1940-2011).

Thundery Showers is by far Smith's most mature work. It oozes a degree of confidence. The novel is a work ahead of its time, outside time. She captures every nuance of a dreary seaside town; the dashed hopes of a day on the beach, the families sheltering from the rain in shop doorways, the –

Katia closed the book.

"Oh, Deborah! You are so cynical!"

Something was missing. There was no smell of lavender. Katia got up from the table.

"Excuse me, have you seen Deborah Smith in here today?"

The man behind the counter didn't answer, lost in the procedure of fixing together parts of his coffee-making apparatus.

"I'm looking for Deborah Smith," said Katia. "Floppy hat. Little round glasses. Big black umbrella. Has she been in?"

He balanced two flathead screws on the counter, taking his time to reply.

"Having a laugh, are you?"

"Sorry?"

"I'm not being funny, but this café's a business, not a refuge for waifs and strays. You've come in three times this week and not spent a single penny. Not even a cup of tea. You just slink over to the corner and hide behind your book, talking to yourself. I see everything that goes on in here, you know."

"But not Deborah Smith?"

"Who?"

"I'll have the full English breakfast, please. Tick every box on the chit for me. Give me the lot. And a pot of tea. If you could bring it all over?"

Katia returned to her place in the corner. She hoped Deborah hadn't decided their business together was finished. After all, a book signing event was only one step up on the ladder. But maybe that was all that *Sunny with a Moderate Breeze* needed. Indeed, Katia's first novel was a step in itself.

"Belle? Are you there?"

Katia knew how to spark Belle's interest. She needed a peer. An equal. Katia was prepared to rise to the challenge. There was only one thing to do. She would have to write another book.

Appreciation

This light, pleasant and playful story evokes the solitude and struggle of the aspiring writer's life. The seaside town and atmosphere of the cafe and bookshop are nicely drawn. The ghost of the dead writer in the cafe is a fun idea, giving writers the moral support we often need.

Unrequited Love by Tony Domaille

Jim worshipped Alice from afar. It had to be from a distance because the last time he had got within range she had threatened to punch him. So, he stared across the care home common room at the object of his devotion, ready to look quickly away if she noticed.

He had to keep an eye out for the care home staff as well, because he'd had a warning for stalking. They hadn't got the police involved but he'd been assertively told that he couldn't –

Declare his love for Alice daily, either directly to her or to other residents.

Hang around the corridor to her room in the hopes of seeing her.

Use the Royal Mail to write her anonymous love letters (because it was obvious it was him.)

Offer her ice cream, toffees, or special biscuits through third parties.

Jim thought these conditions were draconian, but he didn't want to be evicted from the care home, so worshipping from afar was the best he could get. It was killing him, though. Alice was the most beautiful human being he had seen in all his seventy-seven years.

The light blue rinse in her hair shimmered under the fluorescent light strips. The ruby red lipstick she wore made the mouth he so wanted to kiss almost too gorgeous to see. And then there were those eyes, sparkling behind the thick lenses of her spectacles that magnified their allure.

"I hope you're not staring at Alice again."

The voice of Cathy, the entertainments officer, made him break his fix on Alice. "No, he lied. I'm just interested in the different things the ladies are creating in the knit and natter session."

Cathy grinned. "Of course you are. Maybe I could fetch you some needles and wool so you can have a go."

"Er, no thanks." Jim shook his head. "I should be getting along."

He took one last longing look at the octogenarian of his dreams and slunk out of the common room. If he couldn't look at Alice, Scrabble in the games room with a cup of tea might distract him, so that's where he headed.

Playing Scrabble with George was a challenge. He claimed he had Tourette's and wasn't responsible for any bad language he produced with the tiles. He also claimed that maths wasn't his strong point, and that's why he invariably under-recorded his opponent's score. But what George lacked in parlour game decorum, he made up for in being supportive.

"Did you get thrown out of the common room?" George asked as Jim sat heavily opposite him.

"No, but I was staring at Alice again,"

George nodded. "You really do have it bad for her, don't you? Now me, I'm more than sweet on Leanne."

"Leanne?"

"Yes."

"The girl in the kitchen?"

"That's the one."

Jim shook his head. "She's only about twenty years old."

George paused in his placing of a disgusting four-letter word on the scrabble board. "See, I'd have put her mid-twenties. I'll tell you, mate, if I were seventy years younger... By the way, are you going on the trip to Weston-Super-Mare?"

"Might as well," said Jim, miserably.

"I expect Alice will go." George put a word on the board that Jim thought you could be arrested for. "Hey, imagine. If it's a sunny day, she might take off that thick cardy she always wears. That'll get your blood racing, eh?"

***

Jim was first on the coach on the day of the trip to Weston. The care home staff thought putting him on before anyone else meant they could get Alice aboard without any danger of him engineering a seat close to her. They were right, of course, but it meant he could sit right at the back and have a perfect view of the vision that was Alice when she stepped on.

The sun was out. George's prediction that Alice would leave her cardigan was spot on. She climbed onto the coach in a floral dress, with her hair perfectly set and makeup just right. Jim's heart rate went up and he was sure the sight of her made his blood pressure condition infinitely worse. Then she sat next to her friend Joan, and he couldn't see anything beyond her headrest.

All the way to Weston, Jim wondered why he was even going. He knew he'd only booked because of Alice, but it all seemed so futile once they were travelling. He wasn't allowed anywhere near her. So, when the coach pulled into the car park, and the long process of marrying foldaway mobility scooters and Zimmer frames with two thirds of the travellers began, Jim thought he might not bother to get off.

"Come on, mate, shift yourself," said George, suddenly appearing. "They've got a Wetherspoons just round the corner. We can get on the scotch for pennies."

"I think I'll just stay here," said Jim, but George grabbed his arm and pulled him to his feet.

"You're not sitting on the coach for the day, mooning over unrequited love. Come on."

As they got off, Jim could see Alice walking arm in arm with Joan just a few yards ahead of them. What he wouldn't give to have Alice's arm through his.

"Stick with me," said George. "We'll have a fine old time."

And then it happened. It all seemed to be in slow motion to Jim, but he saw the hooded youth on a bicycle heading toward the line of elderly people and knew instantly something wasn't right. The boy and bike were too close and as they flashed by Alice, he saw the kid reach out and wrench Alice's handbag right off her shoulder. He saw her stagger, feared she would fall. He heard her startled cry and the cries of those around her and the bike was almost level with him and George. He knew what he had to do and just threw himself at the bike.

There were more alarmed cries as Jim, bike, and youth crashed to the ground.

"Ooof! You old git." The pole-axed kid was obviously winded.

"I'll clip your bloody ears," said Jim, snatching back Alice's bag and pulling himself to his feet.

And then the boy picked up his bike and peddled off fast, while everyone was around Jim, applauding him, and slapping him on the back.

"Good man."

"You showed that little bugger."

"Are you okay? That was quite a clash."

Jim could feel the bruises forming, but adrenaline was masking any pain. And then all his dreams came true as Alice came through the crowd and flung her arms around him.

"Jim, Jim, are you hurt? That was so brave."

She released him from her lavender scented hug, and he felt giddy. "Here's your bag," he said.

Alice stood looking into his eyes. "I'm glad to have it back, but I'm much more concerned about you. That was heroic."

He shrugged. "Well, I'm glad to have helped, but I'm not supposed to talk to you so…'

Alice hugged him again, and whispered in his ear, "I've been a very silly old woman. How could I have complained that you care so much about me?"

Jim felt a warm glow and saw George smile and wink at him.

"We should get you checked over," said Alice.

"I'm fine, really."

"You're sure?

"Sure."

Alice looked into his eyes again, seemingly checking the truth of what he said, and then uttered words he had never dreamed he would hear. "Then, I hope you'll come and have a drink with me, Jim, so I can say a proper thank you. I want you to tell me all about yourself. I want to hear all about my hero."

Appreciation

This funny story gives us a picture of romantic love, not in youth, as usual, but in age. It plays with the mild entertainments and anticipated dullness of care home life, breathing passion into them and letting us laugh along with a heroic fantasy. Jim and George are a charming, wry pair, and no word is wasted; there is a smile or a laugh in every line. Alice is a beauty, and able to change her mind. What a hopeful vision: with a little courage, unrequited love can become shared passion, even towards the end of life.

Mark of Approval by Angela Nansera

Mark vapes beside a No Smoking sign. Tilts his head back. Siphons the dregs from a packet of crisps. He tracks me stepping off the bus and racing towards him, the weeks of stress stretch across his face. *Must Hurry*. Not because he was missed. Or that his mother lies ill upstairs. But to get this over and done with. Ten minutes tops should do it. In. Out, with enough time to catch the nine fifteen. Reaching the hospital entrance, the mist from his e-cigarette lingers, slow to fade in the morning sun.

Hands in jeans, he flounces through doors. Trundling behind, a corridor the shade of mental health green boasts a food hall, pharmacy and shop selling crocheted dream catchers. This is my first time back in years. Before our visits to Bristol were always by car and always with Mark. After nights out he would stay with his parents and me elsewhere. "It's easier this way," he would say, before, "Penny, we talked about this," my silence accepted as mutual consent. Born with blemishes covering the whole of my body had made his parents reject me, and after dropping Mark off, the kind eyes of friends would flicker against harsh streetlights in the cab back to theirs.

From their top floor flat, the red-lit eyes of Brandon Hill tower failed to reveal Mark's whereabouts, our families distant and dissimilar, but both in the habit of protecting their own.

He calls for the lift. "You're late."

"Eight minutes thirteen, to be exact." We step inside. "Your city buses have village timetables."

"When I say late," he says, his breath a mix of onion and chemical grape, "I don't mean just now."

"You're lucky I'm here at all." Reaching out, he pulls away. "How's your mum?"

"Still alive. Still asking for you."

"And … your dad?"

"You watered my sunflowers?"

"Christ, Mark, I've not seen you for weeks, back in London paying *your* bills and you're wittering on about your triffids."

"I did thank you … on the phone."

"'Cheers mate' in a text does not equate explicit gratitude to your partner of ten years. And yes, your slug slurpers have grown ten per cent."

His usual response that beauty is everywhere if you look hard enough is replaced by a grunt; a mantra not applying to his in-laws, who since discovering my existence had rejected me like corrupt data. Their rebuff appeared to be based on their country's history of capturing and controlling pretty much everywhere else, my inferiority established by past generations long before. My morning ritual of repeating positive affirmations into a mirror never materialised into a surge of acceptance. All that reflected was a continent. Dark. Rugged. Torn. Maybe that explains my lack of career progression as an assistant accountant, transferring income from bank statements onto various spreadsheets. If this sounds dull, you'd be wrong. Maths is fun. Multiply twenty-five thousand two hundred by the five seconds it took to describe my job, and you have the sum total of my working week.

We shunt upwards, the floor number displayed above lift doors lighting up in turn. The mechanical cage stops. Fills and empties; patients, visitors, staff. Some have similar markings to mine, in varying shades. Safety in numbers. Compared to words they are less ambiguous; leave less room for doubt in a world judging me at face value. Words on the other hand are open to interpretation, hours wasted debating their meaning, capturing each syllable as if holding it up for ransom. Mark once compared my personality to a child's paddling pool; shallow on the surface, with depth if pushed.

Fifteenth floor. The lift opens and trailing after hunched shoulders, we reach a single ward at the end of the hall, its door ajar.

She looks up from the bed. Hatred and ignorance flanked by screens and vials. Loitering on the edge, my unease grows.

"Mum," says Mark approaching, "you've not touched breakfast."

She scowls at the toast. Takes his hand. Asks what the outside is doing. He replaces what he might usually say – traffic, heatwave, lunch – with, "Mum, this is Penny."

Eyes sallow and bloodstained stare with an intensity impossible to look away from. She talks about me to Mark. *Hello. I am standing here.* Is this the definition of compassion? Not donating to charities or extending a deadline to colleagues to find a month-end balance difference, but agreeing to meet a pickle-faced woman with days to live whose husband also despised me because of the colour of my skin?

She shoos Mark away. Tells him to grab a coffee. Does she want anything? "You *knows* what I want," she says, her accent thick. He says she's not allowed that anymore and she talks over him when reminded it was years of drinking that got her there in the first place. He shuts the door. It seems to take all her energy to pull herself up, gnarly fingers beckoning me close.

"He'll not be long," she says, voice laboured. "He's a good lad. Kind. *Wise*."

"Except with his choice of partner."

"You've cut your hair."

"They were braids."

"They hid your features …."

That photo. The infamous selfie taken ten years ago that outed me; collecting student ID cards in Fresher's week, Mark catching one of my stray hair extensions between his teeth. Explaining why my false hair had long since been removed, replaced by various styles – twists, cornrows, relaxed, weave and back to natural – would lead to more questions loathed to divulge.

"… You have such striking features. What does your dad do?"

"Rents flats."

"And your mum?"

"In the picture somewhere, but on the edge of the frame."

"And your extraction?"

"My what?"

"Where. Are. You. From?"

"Brix.Ton."

She circles her finger around my face.

"Uganda, if that's what you're asking."

She winces, as if recalling the image of the former military president, Idi Amin, her only association with this country, like France is known for cheese. She rubs a distended belly as the DJ announces *Before the Deluge* by Jackson Browne. The air thickens, her energy undiluted by the droning song. She gestures, edging me closer to sit on a chair. Outside, when asking Mark if his dad was coming, he had said, "Not if you are," then further interrogated the wellbeing of his plants as if they had been separated by war and given up for adoption. Apart from his gardening obsession and this in-law conflict, we had bumbled along; an item since the infamous *Guess Who's Coming to Dinner* snap, our first three years butting against students thrashing around campus in shoals, clinging onto each other in some post-adolescent grip, attending meals, gigs, each other's rooms and lectures, friends convinced our union a write off as so incompatible. When once asked to describe my love language, (obvious that from the five Mark's was 'touch'), my response? A sixth; likened to the 'quiet carriage' of a high-speed train; all noise kept to a minimum and calls taken outside.

What possessed me to come back? A stranger in a strange place, an audience with a woman rebuking my permanent tattoo. If born in *her* shade, would my pre-judged viewpoint be like hers? Growing up my parents had spoken to one another in their mother tongue and to me only in English. Not understanding conversations meant deciphering interactions through nonverbal cues, straddling two worlds at home and outside, belonging to neither. A halfway house that hurt. Dating Mark, my sense of not fitting in manifested itself in shame, grateful for any attention even if ill-received, feeling like the most expensive doll in the shop, played with but never bought. But Mark did buy me, accusations accruing ever since that choosing him made me a sellout. He had never thought to warn his parents of my *birth defect* before sharing the Freshers' week shot. "We live in modern times," he had said, "people are people are people," their initial shock never dissolving to remove the need to sleep on friend's floors. Did he ever challenge them? He would dismiss my explanation that markings matter, you blend or bleed, fit in or stick out, accuse me of exaggerating; *he* had never experienced racism, so it couldn't be *that* bad. But rules matter. Take Excel. Input the wrong syntax, space or formula inside a cell and it always returns an error.

She leans towards the radio. Smiles. Geometric web-like veins radiate beneath the feint crimson hues on the cheek that took the fall. She sings. Murmurs like prayers. Something about nature revealing our secrets, our inner light dwindling as we reach sky-bound when it's our time. A delicate, liver-spotted hand stretches. Wraps itself around mine. Then Mark waltzes in, a rod of energy rendering her upright, her clasp revealing everything in the squeeze of her grip.

***

"It's best you don't come to the funeral."

"You said."

"It's the family—'

"Mark, you said. We've never met—'

"It'd be awkward …."

We had not spoken in days. Not since he barged in, broke us up, never saying why.

She had taken my hand. Skin powdery and delicate and lingering around mine. Hazy eyes plunged me deep, beyond egg-white eye lids, suspended inside her vast, expansive vortex, comforted by her touch. *Before the Deluge* seeped from the radio in undulating waves, her clutch lasting an eternity, until Mark broke our hold.

"Mum. Whatcha doing—?"

"Mark … calm down, we were talking—'

He lowered his voice. "Let's get you comfortable." Planting a polystyrene cup into soggy bread, he tidied her pillow. Adjusted her hair. Turned the radio up. "Mum. Remember? Your favourite?"

"Course," she had said, tone conciliatory. "Sounds familiar … but—'

"It's *Nothing Compares 2 U*. I requested it."

"Son … this isn't Sinead O'Connor."

Hands tingling, the room returned to view. "It's Prince."

She stared. "He doing covers now—?"

"He wrote the original. My dad has it on vinyl."

"To be fair he's probably skint. Not had a hit in years—'

"Because he's dea—"

Mark blocked her from view. "You'll confuse her."

Bolting from the windowless room, crazy jade walls guided me into the lift. Breath blurring, the craft descended, floor numbers pulsed. Alien. Jagged. Doors opened and cement feet dragged along the ground floor, past that shop selling culturally misappropriate woven hoops and smocks made from sustainably sourced yak wool. *Must. Hurry.* Clambering inside a no-bus Uber, my return train was caught just in time, our first conversation days later, Mark acting as if what had happened didn't matter when it mattered to me.

"… Least you're taking my calls."

Silence.

"Penny … how are things at home?"

"Sorry about your mum."

"You said. Although '*my condolences*' in a text does not … how did you put it … equate to explicit gratitude to your partner of ten years."

"Mark, let's not."

"Let's."

"OK. Why keep me hidden?"

"When?"

"In Bristol … your parents –?"

"You said it was OK –'

Silence.

"Penny. We agreed –'

"I couldn't handle the conflict."

"Families have backstories starting long before you entered the scene."

Unease floods. Pressure in the gut. Not stabbing. Or heaving. But an ache so dull it originates from a source, cavernous, impossible to reach, a throb not soothed by calming hands. "I honoured your mum's wishes. Maintained my dignity and you flounced in like the birthday kid who's lost Pass the Parcel."

"My parents were … are from a different time."

"And we no longer burn witches."

"What?"

"Ignorance is no excuse not to change," reminding him what his mum had said when we first arrived, her surprise at my colouring – darker than their neighbour who, "Isn't she mulatto of some form?", before comparing Mark to their cousin who, "also had a taste for the blacks." And Mark had laughed in that way he did as if caught red-handed mixing darks with a white wash. It was as much my fault. Failing to intervene due to shock and learnt acceptance of a lack of power to challenge.

He clears his throat. "Mum was just repeating what Dad always says. She didn't mean –"

"Why do I always have to preserve fragilities, take the higher ground? We were … making headway."

"She was tired –"

"She was making a connection."

"Pen, why bring this up now? With everything that has happened … Maybe her liking you might have made her like me less."

Bulbous sobs churn inside the handset. Him walking in, spotting our possible reconciliation, the ignited flash of resentment and realisation of the years he had wasted neglecting his mum's needs. That's the problem with words; they are not final like closing balances, they are open to interpretation, misunderstanding. Her touch felt like an equation. It had sides. Balance. Resolution.

It added up.

***

Irises reaching their peak shelter the geraniums. Watering Mark's flowers reminds me of how he *always* sees colour when gardening but never with us. How can he plant an herbaceous border for maximum effect – marigolds, asters, delphiniums, daisies, their petal numbers following Fibonacci's mathematic sequence – but not apply the same logic in the acknowledgment of our racial divide? Entwining her hands in mine felt like a sacred request for forgiveness that words never could. She had asked to meet. Not because *she* hated me. But because *her husband did*, his dominant narrative doing whatever it took to protect *his* kind. Just like my dad. Visiting one of his houses in my first year of uni, him recommending an album from his vintage vinyl stack. Gazing through the window, he had spotted Mark. Peered. Yanked me upstairs. Banged on his tenants' doors, demanding answers from those daring to open. "Tell my daughter what colour she is," he had said, barking, spitting. A trick question? An answer so obvious that if confirming my blackness would be the wrong answer and he would raise their rent? The rage behind calm eyes burned with memories of a loathing to his own markings, convinced my future destined to not evolve if Mark and my species mixed. The opposite of love is not hate. It's fear. Fear of power. Of gaining it. Losing it. Of consequence. Reputation. That's what our parents fought for. To maintain order. Protect it. Stick to your own. Accept the 'as is'. That's what her clasp in mine did. It transcended the tangle of words, confirming that nature's governance is not determined by some socially constructed hierarchy, but by a grand design greater than the sum of our parts.

***

Mark waits for my signal. Safety belt fastened, he starts the car.

"Sure you want to come?" he says. Sensing my nod, he pulls away.

"Even if they—

"Who cares?" Smoothing his morning suit translates to thanking him for coming to collect me. "What others think of me no longer counts."

We merge onto the M4. Ink splattered sketches of migrating birds dot the azure sky. No borders, or exclusions, our return journey familiar. He tells me over a purring engine the word familiar comes from family. If he navigates within fifty-five and sixty-five miles per hour, the car will operate at its most efficient for fuel economy. With a sunny forecast, no scheduled delays, we should arrive in Bristol thirteen minutes earlier than un-expected to pay our last respects.

Appreciation

This touching story confronts the complexities of racism and the effort to establish one's own identity in the face of it. There is a balance of ethnocentric antipathy, in the sense that both Penny's father and her in-laws reject her relationship with Mark. The language is fast-moving, associative, poetic, reproducing the rapidity of thought and sensation. The plants and the Excel sheets are deployed as telling images, embodying modes of thought, domains of colour and consideration that echo the story's themes: ways of seeing, ways of thinking. Questions are raised about the reliability of language. The wisdom of the piece lies in its demonstration that courage and an awareness of our own mortality can resolve the differences between people, recalling us to our shared humanity.

The Medusa Effect by Suki Broad

The TV told me the world is ending.

"A massive stellar flyby is predicted to move the earth's orbit off by mere centimetres, meaning the destruction of all life as we know it." Says news anchor Jonathan from behind his mahogany desk. Even in the face of imminent death he still manages to utilise that dazzling presenter smile.

He's the kind of minor celebrity that everyone's mum goes crazy for. With a chiselled jawline, periwinkle eyes hiding behind Clark Kent style spectacles, and a deep voice that leaves you wondering if he went through puberty twice. He's the perfect man to break the news of our impending extinction.

In a moment of staged sincerity, Jonathan whips his spectacles from the pronounced bridge of his nose and gives the camera his best concerned – but still immaculate – gaze. "We may not have long, and it's moments like these that bring us face to face with what truly matters. Which is why we want to thank you, our loyal viewers, for your patronage! Now back to Joel for sports…"

I leave it running and set off the kettle. I guess this means it's too late to get a cat. I've been going back and forth on the idea for several months, but I can never seem to commit. The tea turns a cloudy brick red as I stir in the milk. The cat could have been that colour too, a nice dark ginger teabag purring in my lap. It could have been just what this place needs. Just a little more life.

In the days that follow, a rumble of panic spreads through the neighbourhood. At first, it's just a couple of people who are taking stock in the initial coverage – the doomsday preparers, the overly anxious believers, the ready-for-anything-ers, but it doesn't take long for everyone else to come to terms with the reality of it all. We are going to die. And there's nothing we can do to stop it. There's no defence great enough, no missile big enough, no superhero from any comic book real enough to stop what's about to happen.

My neighbour's eyes lock onto mine as I bump into him in the hallway, a suitcase in one hand, flowers in the other. A single bead of sweat drips from his balding temple as he fixes his gaze ahead of him, muttering under his breath, "I'm coming my love. I'm coming…"

Gradually, they all trickle from their apartments, flooding the stairwell and the streets below. My fingers curl around my warm mug as I peer down from my third-floor apartment. The entire road is quickly congested with honking cars and lonesome figures that weave their way through the traffic, trailing suitcases behind them. The fleeing civilians leave an apocalyptic scene in their wake; grocery bags spinning in the wind, a child's teddy bear dropped and left on the side of the road, abandoned vehicles with their engines still running. Some are left with their doors wide open, mid-swing. No one will ever close them.

Where on earth were they even running to? I take a sip of my tea and munch on a custard cream. The shop on the corner had been abandoned shortly after the news, leaving the defenceless biscuits ripe for the taking. I nabbed a few packets of Jammie Dodgers as well, but I'm saving those for a special occasion.

"Stuffing your face with tea and biscuits. Honestly, I don't know how you haven't blown up like a balloon yet." That's what my mum would say. She hates how many biscuits I eat. Well, guess what mum? It's the end of the world. We're all about to blow up, and my biscuits had nothing to do with it. *"One of these days you're going to have to learn how to cook some real food."* I do know how to cook, thank you very much. To a middling quality, sure, but I'm not helpless. Besides, I live in the middle of the city, so most nights I eat out. And I like to save cupboard space for things that are truly important. Like biscuits.

Biscuits aside, mum and I couldn't be more different if we tried. I work admin for some firm where my boss doesn't even know my name, whereas mum is at the top of her field running projects, speaking at conferences, and flying all over the world. She specialises Greek mythology and is passionate and proud of her work. The last time I had pride in anything was when I was five and made a Medusa doll out of playdough, and that was only because it made mum ecstatic.

"Just look at that hideous face!" She cooed, gently prodding one of the crooked green snake-hairs that I'd skilfully crafted. The playdough was slightly dry, so her deadly yellow eyes kept falling off, but mum didn't care. "It's perfect!" She had said to me. "A Gorgon monster made by my little monster."

I can't remember the last time she called me her little monster. Nowadays she just refers to me as…well, we'd moved past the age of pet names. Then some time ago we moved past phone calls, to sporadic texts, to only seeing each other on the holidays, to barely acknowledging each other's existence.

I guess time is kind of like trying to fight Medusa. You have to keep moving, keep busy, stop watching and start doing because if you just stand and stare as time passes you by, she'll catch you, and you'll eventually turn to stone. That's what my relationship with mum is like now. Stone.

Jonathan is back on the screen, and he has a friend – I mean colleague – with him this time. It's Suzanne who does the weather. She's always a bundle of laughs.

"Suzanne, as our resident meteorologist I'm sure you're just itching to tell everyone your opinion on the recent astronomical happenings."

"It's certainly more interesting to talk about than the rain we've been having all week."

They both force a laugh.

"Well, don't hold back on my account. Care to predict what will happen over the next few days? Dramatic weather? Increased seismic activity? Maybe even fire raining down from the heavens?"

"Oh, nothing like that. This isn't some Hollywood movie. When we go it's going to be much less dramatic." Says Suzanne. "What really interests me is the social changes we're going to see over the next few days as the end draws closer."

"Social changes?"

"Yes. To be frank, I think we're going to notice a dramatic increase in people who just stop giving a fuck."

Jonathan's perfectly sculpted smile falters. "I beg your pardon, Suzanne?"

"You heard me, Jonathan. In fact, we have several reports coming in on this very phenomenon as we speak. Mass walkouts across multiple large corporations, riots in the streets, and a small town in Yorkshire has closed themselves off and started their own purge society. There really is nothing like the end of the world to bring out the worst in humanity, am I right?" Suzanne cackles obscenely. It's a glorious noise that is nothing like the usual weather-girl giggle she puts on when Jonathan makes a throwaway sexist comment about the length of her skirt.

"It sounds like you've really done your homework there, Suzanne. But we should really get back to your subject of expertise now."

"I'm not a meteorologist, Jonathan. I have a degree in sociology. And you'd know that if you'd ever talked to me instead of my tits. That's the only reason they gave me this job in the first place, right? Because of my tits. And at first, I thought, hey, easy money. But you know what? I hate my job. I hate this studio. I hate that food cart with those awful sandwiches that taste like feet. And most of all, I hate you, Jonathan. I'm almost glad that the end of the world is happening so I can finally tell you and everyone else at this sad news station to fuck off. This is Suzanne, signing off."

She throws her mic down, flips off the camera, and leaves. Jonathan's jaw is left hanging from its hinges, just like the still open door Suzanne stormed through. The poor guy is probably scrambling to find something witty to say, but before he can, they cut to commercial.

My half-dunked biscuit breaks off into my tea bringing me back to my living room. I look down at the soggy mixture just in time to witness the disintegrating biscuit chunk bob twice and sink to the bottom of the mug. You know what? Forget about the Custard Creams. It's time to open the Jammie Dodgers.

For all his flaws, I could sympathise with Jonathan. Just a little. I'd been yelled at like that only once before in my life, by my ex. We'd been dating for all of eight months when he asked me if I wanted to try out this new swanky coffee-slash-bakery that had just opened, specialising in baked goods made from some special pumpkin flour. I, who like neither coffee nor pumpkin, told him I'd pass.

"But it won't even taste like pumpkin. It's just the flour they use, and you don't have to order coffee, you can order juice, or tea, or whatever you want."

But that isn't the point. Why should I trek all the way to some café where they're going to overcharge me for tea when I can have it for free right here? I told him as much.

Two flared nostrils and one hard, cold stare later, he ended things with me. Explosively.

"I'm not going to stick around here until I become part of the furniture." He had howled. *"There's more to the world than sitting around in this dusty flat all day. I have my whole life to live. My whole fucking life."* Similar to Suzanne, he'd stormed out without bothering to shut the door. Rude.

His number's still on my phone, listed under the name *pumpkin wanker*. I could call him, tell him that I've had a change of heart, that I'd be happy to visit the stupid café with him and eat the stupid pumpkin treats and drink the stupid overpriced coffee. It's never too late to reschedule, is it?

I lick a stray crumb from my lip as a coffee commercial I've already seen a thousand times plays. My phone rests on the seat beside me, but I don't reach for it. Its blank screen catches against the lamp's cold white light and from this angle I can see all the fingerprints that litter its surface. Every groove on each dusty imprint spirals inwards, coiling around each other until they finally meet in the centre.

I have a bunch of fossils that look kind of like that under my bed. Ammonites. I hadn't thought about them in years. As a kid, my dad took me to a beach that was littered with ammonite fossils, and I'd be forced to hunt for them until I dropped from exhaustion. It was his idea of father-daughter bonding time. In truth, I'd always had a feeling that mum put him up to it, and in retaliation he chose a bonding activity that would be the most effort-free on his part. Not that I ever had a say in it.

I'd scour for hours, digging through the sand, turning over every stone until the sea came back in and chased me away. I'd twist them over in my hands, simultaneously in love with them for their beauty and despising them for being so arduous to collect. "The best things come with hard work," my dad would drone from under his parasol, the latest bestselling crime-thriller open in his lap.

I guess he was right. Take a fossil for instance, a perfect shell encased in carbon with each ridge and groove perfectly preserved after thousands of years of immense pressure.

I always found enough to fill bucket-loads, and I'd fall in love with each and every fossil that I found. But dad only ever let me keep the perfect ones, and no matter how much I cried or begged, he always threw the uglies back in the sea. They sank to their watery graves along with my hard work, never to be found again.

The so-called perfect specimens now collect dust under my bed, and the last thing that crawled out from there had eight hairy legs. I haven't been brave enough to have a look since.

I pick up my phone and run a thumb over the cold glass screen. I scan my contacts list – mum, dad, *pumpkin wanker* – and hover my thumb precariously over the bright green phone icon. With the slightest of movements, I twitch and hit the mark.

Fuck it.

Before the dial tone starts, I hang up and shove my phone into the pocket of my nightgown. I doubt they'd even pick up anyway.

I tip my mug and down the last of my tea. The bottom is stained a rusty brown and as hard as I tried, I could never get it clean. With a sigh, I heave myself off the sofa, and trudge back to the kitchen. The kettle crackles to life.

"Once again, I implore you all to reach out to your loved ones..." Jonathan looks different today. Gone is the sharp man in a suit and spectacles. He now wears a loose, wrinkled shirt and a careless grin. "I wanted to let you know that this is the last you'll be seeing of me. From here on out I'll be spending the final moments of my existence with my beautiful family." He adjusts his papers, smacks the edges against the table until they form a neat stack before promptly throwing them all behind him. I thought that the papers would scatter once they were tossed and flutter softly around him like some bizarre corporate version of confetti. But they rise and fall together, meeting the ground with a thwump.

Jonathan continues: "And since it doesn't matter anymore, I wanted to tell anyone still watching this news channel that you're a waste of space. Seriously, don't you have anything better to do with your final days alive than sit on your couch feeling sorry for yourself? I'm going to do what I should have done days ago, maybe even years ago, and get a life. Thank God I'm not you."

And with that he leaves, the camera still filming an empty desk. An awkward pause. "We'll be right back after these messages..." someone says off-camera.

But nothing comes back. The rest of the team must have followed suit after Jonathan's outburst, because all that remains of the channel is static. I hug my empty tea mug and watch the little black and white dots dance on the screen for a few moments longer before finally turning it off.

I freeze at the site of my own reflection. I'm tiny and unkempt in my oversized dressing gown, my skin is grey in the cold lighting, and my back is hunched from slouching for far too long. I'm sitting in the middle of a sofa meant for three. There's a lamp to my left. A fern next to that. My coffee table is bare except for a set of unused coasters, and hundreds of concentric white rings stained into the wood over many years of misuse. Unable to withstand my own gaze any longer, I look down at my toes. Wriggle them. Not stone yet.

I blink, an empty mug still in my hands, a celestial object just moments away from crashing into me veering me even further off course. There's no Jonathan, no roaring kettle or hot tea to soften the blow. The world will be swept into the frigid emptiness of space, and everyone will freeze, turning into statues within seconds. Our final moments will be preserved for the ages. Parents cradling their babies, desperate lovers entwined, families locked in one final embrace. And then there'll be me, alone on a couch, not cradling a baby, or a cat, or a lover, but an empty mug.

Appreciation

We are at the end of the world, people are descending into panic and shedding their fake appearances, and the narrator is unperturbed. The tone is sharp, funny, and the details are vivid. We learn the origin of her psychological state: parents who didn't see her. The Medusa effect of the title is both the mass turning to stone to be caused by the impending catastrophe, and the mother's failure or inability to nurture her child. The girl made a playdough Medusa, aligning with her mother's interests. Only then was she appreciated. Her father also seems indifferent, demanding perfection in the ammonites, and in her, while himself distracted by a crime novel. This neglect causes the melancholic narrator's attitude of gloomy fatalism, compounded by her rejection of superficial café and sexist TV culture, and creates her final pathos, holding a stained and empty mug. It's almost a relief that everyone is doomed. Perhaps she needs to make a psychological break from her parents, accept herself, and find something worth striving for that aligns with her authentic identity and values. But then the end is coming anyway. Does the story also echo the climate crisis, another apocalypse? It captures something important about the condition of this generation.

The Added Bonus of an Off Switch
by Claire Jaggard

Rosemary Norbridge resembled a cabbage. As wide as she was short, time had folded deep creases into her face and despite vigorous brushing, her hair crinkled into layers that refused to lie flat.

"Just look at me, Mrs Pringle," she was saying. "You can see I'm not Stella."

Edith Pringle placed her teacup back on its saucer.

'My eyes may not be as keen as they were, Miss Norbridge, but there's nothing wrong with my ears, and what I hear is pure Stella Logan."

Rosemary suppressed a sigh, sinking a little deeper into the chintz-covered sofa.

She'd first become aware of Mrs Pringle a couple of weeks previously, at the end of a working week that had wrapped up, as it always did, with the show's catchphrase:

"… and remember, always trust your instinct!"

The actors had laughed as their signature tune faded up under the sound effect of cocktail glasses clinking. The producer had flicked off the studio's red light and leant on the talkback button.

"Well done folks, another episode in the bag."

Rosemary had gathered up her knitting and followed her on-air husband through the soundproof doors. The bald patch on the back of his head was larger than it used to be and his shirt collar frayed at the edges. What would the listeners think if they could see how the suave hero of *Ralph Logan's Adventures* looked in real life? What, indeed, would they think of her?

The secretary had been waiting for her in the corridor, brandishing a letter.

"You'll like this one, Miss Norbridge. One of your fans wants to remember you in her will."

Rosemary had noted the heavy quality of the paper, the neatness of the handwriting and the clarity of the message. Mrs Edith Pringle intended to leave Rosemary her entire estate, and wished her to know in advance so she could take the bequest into account when planning her future.

Was it wishful thinking, tiredness after a long day… or just weakness? Rosemary was usually wary of listener correspondence, but something told her Edith Pringle was not a typical show devotee. The letter contained no gushing prose, no heavy underlining, not even a request for an autograph. There was, however, only one appropriate response.

"Tell her 'thank you, but no thank you'."

A week later the secretary had reappeared.

"She still wants to leave you her money. Should we send her your shot?"

Rosemary grimaced. She wasn't vain, but her cabbage-like appearance in the latest set of publicity photographs had been a disappointment.

"If we must, we must."

Listeners who tuned in to their radios each Friday night knew Rosemary as Stella, Ralph Logan's adoring wife and plucky sidekick. Stella Logan deployed feminine wiles in crystalline tones and attracted fan mail by the sackload.

The Logans' fictional lifestyle revolved around foreign travel, fine restaurants and fast cars, buoyed by a rousing orchestral theme. Each episode opened on a note of high energy, peaked at a moment of peril and ended by unpicking the plot over cocktails, in case any listener might not have been paying close attention.

Real life for Rosemary Norbridge was far less glamorous; she spent her days reading scripts, recording in windowless studios and knitting scarves for other cast members when not needed at the microphone. The only hint of drama came from the constant fear of losing her job. Rosemary had landed the part of Stella in her mid-thirties and by sheer good fortune, her cut glass received pronunciation still maintained its youthful qualities twenty years later. Her leading men had not been so lucky; Rosemary was now on her third make-believe husband.

She knew her voice would betray her eventually. The call from management would come, a younger actress would step in and Rosemary would be shown the door. Mrs Pringle might be thinking of Rosemary's future; Rosemary herself preferred not to.

The third time the secretary had appeared, she'd simply shrugged her shoulders and flapped the latest missive from Mrs Pringle.

Enough was enough. Appealing though the idea of a windfall might be, Rosemary felt it simply wouldn't do to take someone's money on the basis of an illusion. She'd instructed the secretary to send a telegram announcing her intention to visit in person.

The following day Rosemary had boarded the 2:10 from Paddington, changed at Reading, then allowed herself the rare luxury of a taxi to Edith Pringle's wisteria-clad cottage.

Now the two ladies sat eye to eye over a Victoria sandwich and a pot of Earl Grey.

"It's very kind of you, but I can't possibly accept. Think of your family, Mrs Pringle."

Edith Pringle wafted a dismissive hand.

"My husband died years ago and we weren't blessed with children. Can I tempt you to a piece of cake?"

"You must have other relatives."

"I do, and I wish they came with the added bonus of an off switch. Radio is generally a delight to listen to. They are not."

Rosemary was about to protest further, but Mrs Pringle paused halfway through cutting the cake, her knife hovering above a sprinkling of caster sugar.

"Do you live alone, Miss Norbridge?"

Rosemary nodded.

"Whose is the first voice you hear when you wake up in the morning? And the last before you go to sleep?"

Rosemary thought of the presenters, newsreaders and continuity announcers whose voices filtered through her portable wireless at all hours of the day and night. Her working life was filled with people, but yes, radio drowned out the emptiness at home.

Mrs Pringle plunged her blade back into the sponge.

"Radio is such a comfort. It transports me to other worlds and gives me people to share a joke with; the way you tease Ralph, his digs about your shopping trips and those lovely phrases that keep popping up: "Always trust your instinct!"

Her eyes twinkled as she handed Rosemary the slice of cake.

"Think of the fun we've had! I've drunk pink gins with you, I've shared the thrills of your adventures… and all those wonderful cocktail parties where clever Ralph explains the clues I missed. You have to admit it's been quite a ride."

Despite herself, Rosemary smiled and nodded. Her job was exhausting and poorly paid, but she couldn't imagine having done anything else.

"So you see," continued Mrs Pringle, wiping cake crumbs from her delicate fingers, "you're as good as family, if not better. I never reach for the off switch when *Ralph Logan's Adventures* is on the air. Stella is as real to me as any flesh and blood relative, and indeed, here you are having tea with me!"

"I'm not Stella, Mrs Pringle. It would be lovely if I were, but I'm not."

Mrs Pringle leaned forward.

"I'm going to have to spell this out, aren't I? If anyone is deluded here, Miss Norbridge, it's you. I speak from experience; my husband was an actor too and earned barely enough to feed a hamster. We lived quite comfortably, as you can see, but only because I inherited money. You've had a successful career, but I suspect you've very little put by for when it all ends in a puff of smoke. Am I correct?"

Rosemary put her cake plate on the low table between them. Suddenly she didn't trust herself to hold it steady.

"Miss Norbridge, Stella Logan will outlive us both, but through her you've given me a great deal of pleasure. Let me return the favour. I'm very old and I'd like to die knowing I've helped someone who has shared so much joy."

Rosemary breathed deeply, taking in the room's perfume of beeswax and roses, and allowed herself to relax for the first time in as long as she could remember. Her intuition had been right: Edith Pringle was no ordinary fan, and this was an offer she could not afford to refuse. She pulled herself up straight.

"Mrs Pringle, I will accept your bequest, on one condition."

Edith Pringle lifted an eyebrow.

"Give me your blessing to spend some of the money on my very own 'Ralph Logan Adventure'. I'll travel somewhere exotic where Ralph and Stella have been, I'll wear a ridiculously expensive outfit and I'll raise a pink gin to your memory!"

"Now tell me I'm not having tea with Stella Logan." Mrs Pringle raised her cup in triumph. "Always trust your instinct!"

Rosemary laughed and, this time, the joy was real.

Appreciation

This story is very funny, but also gives a shadow portrait of loneliness. The idea that radio characters could be more real to us than other people in our families is comically absurd yet in a sense true, in that they might fill an emotional space, or need. Our families are often problematic. The names of the characters have a classic English literature ring, like Jane Austen. The physical descriptions and the cabbage photo are very funny, the broadcast context and financial constraints of the characters feel real. The pace is steady, the description uncluttered and clear, locating us firmly in physical scenes. From first to last we trust that we're with an authoritative storyteller. We wonder whether Rosemary Norbridge will finally accept the bequest, and when she does, she in a sense becomes the radio heroine, Stella Logan, completing the play on different forms of reality. The cheerful ending creates a joyful response in the reader, mirroring the emotional reality of the listener, Edith Pringle, in the story.

Night Train by Jon D

Night train night train carry me through the dark
That's me passing in the window, my own little spark
Train lights, poignant, bisecting Carravaggio black
The mighty zing of wheel on rail, never coming back
As silence turns over and settles itself
Once more, under the oldest blanket of night.
Whilst I speed on, deep in my own luxuriant sense
Relentlessly forward but outside time's pretence,
Nothing asked of me nothing required
Dozing reading dreaming is all that has transpired.

From Lagos to Johannesburg, Paris to Milan
Moscow to Vladivostok, Berlin to Amsterdam
Soft human bodies scurry across this dark earth
Tiny creatures hurrying, purpose obscured from birth,
Cross lacing it in skeins of track
Praying that gravity still pulls us back
To the face of this miraculous blue world
Spinning in the emptiness of space
Urging on the night train to help us find our place
Our burrow, each one all alone

Aiming for a place of safety
That we can call a home.
Night train night train carry me through the dark
That's me passing, up there in the window, my own little spark.

Appreciation

The strength of this poem lies in the accuracy of its statement of our human condition and place in the universe. The repetition of 'night train night train', the sweeping lines and the insistent rhyming couplets suggest the sound and feeling of a train's movement. The cities take us all over the world. There is a series of clear images and existential reflections. It's a rational poem that creates an emotional effect.

Contributors

Amy Bacon grew up in rural environments in Malawi and the UK. She moved to Bristol in 2017 to teach English and gained an MA in Creative Writing (with distinction) in 2019. She has previously been published in *Stepaway Magazine*, *Puca Literary Journal*, *The Madrigal Press* and *Spelt Magazine*. She enjoys taking long walks in the city and writing from observation, focusing on the crossovers and connections between humans and nature in the urban environment.

Karen Lewis-Barned, having been an English teacher all her life, marking her students' work, is now writing for herself. She was thoroughly inspired by her Wednesday afternoons at Bristol University exploring how to write memoir. Since then she has written some more and done a few other short writing courses. Stealing from Deborah Levi, she'd like to call her work "Fictional Biography".

H.T. Greatorex mostly writes about misfits and underdogs. When he is not writing he often makes up bedtime stories for his two children. He lives in Bristol.

Celeste Harvey's work has appeared in *Writing History: An Aspects of History Short Story Collection*, plus she was awarded third place in the 2024 Aspects of History Short Story Competition. She is a writer of fiction and memoir and lives in Bristol.

Hilary Smith is a retired teacher from Bristol. She now writes and performs short fiction and creative nonfiction, often inspired by her time in the classroom but also childhood memories and family anecdotes. Her work has been published in *Fictionette*, *Story Attic*, *Writetime* and *Ruler's Wit* and she has performed her stories throughout the South West of England, at literary festivals and on BBC Radio. Her writing is dedicated to her late mum Rita who was a prolific but unpublished author.

Dylan Spicer is a writer specializing in short fiction and transmedia projects, including *The Butter Mouse*, a flash fiction blog that combines storytelling with video, photography, cocktail recipes, and more.

Richard Owen Collins lives in Bristol with his wife and two cats. He teaches Sports Journalism and edits *Tellers* magazine. He's obsessed with writing about entertainment, performativity, addiction, education, travel, and art's place in the modern world. All he wants is to leave the shore of his own mind through a story.

Born on a prison hulk, **Simon Clarke** made an audacious bid for freedom at the age of five, taking refuge with a cut-throat band of river pirates who terrorised the waterways of East Anglia. Eventually back on dry land, he has worked variously at a nuclear plant, a midnight carnival and, lastly and most successfully, at a charming Cotswold tea room where he perfected his recipe for madeira cake. He lives alone with his cats, his grimoires and his memories somewhere in the south west of England.

Rachel Bentham has written drama, docudrama and short stories for broadcast on BBC Radio 4, won prizes for her poetry and scripts, and has collections published by Firewater Press. She enjoys teaching at the Universities of Bristol and Oxford, and is very happy with a pair of good secateurs in her hand.

JM Monaco grew up in Boston, USA and has lived in Bristol since 1996. She has worked in a variety of areas including desk-top publishing and has taught in secondary schools and higher education. Her PhD from the University of Bristol examined quality television and its internet fandom. She has published two novels: *Collision* (2024) and *How We Remember* (2018).

Peter Cowlam writes poetry and prose, and is the literary editor at AN Editions.

Stephen Lang's short fiction has appeared in various collections and anthologies. The latest is *Year of the Tarot – Wands* from Eerie River Publishing. Stephen lives in Bristol with his family.

Tony Domaille writes primarily for the stage, with most of his scripts being published by Lazy Bee Scripts. He was the winner of the Derek Jacobi Award for New Playwriting in 2023. He has also written short stories for a number of print and online magazines and anthologies.

Angela Nansera is a London born, female Afro-British novelist and published short story writer. Her inspiration to write contemporary commercial fiction comes from an innate passion to use storytelling to unravel the complexities of human attachments.

Raised in New Zealand, **Suki Broad** is currently living in Bristol and working as a peer-review editor while sneakily writing fiction under her desk. She's previously had her work published in *Divinations Magazine* and *Bandit Fiction* and is working on a full-length novel.

After thirty years of writing as a broadcast and online journalist, **Claire Jaggard** started scribbling fiction for fun and is always delighted when her short stories are published and broadcast. So far her short stories have been published/broadcast by: *Stroud Short Stories*; *BBC Upload*; *Superpresent*; *Fictionette*; *Secret Attic*; *CafeLit*; *All Your Stories*; and *Egg+Frog*. She is based in Cromhall, South Gloucestershire, and is currently researching ways to commit murder for her first cosy mystery.

Jon D is a recovering academic developing a third career as a writer. His poems are frequently provoked by the shock of finding himself in possession of a bus pass and lurch between unexpected intimacy and utopian activism. He reads regularly on the Bristol open mic scene and has had poems published in *Flight of the Dragonfly*. He also writes short stories.

We hope you enjoyed our first collection. If you'd like to stay in touch, please join our mailing list at: buttondown.com/suspensionspress

Visit us at:
thebristolschoolofwriting.co.uk
suspensionspress.co.uk

Printed in Dunstable, United Kingdom

74796258R00102